CRITICAL
AUTHOR S...
SAVAGE MEMBRANE

"Steve Niles is destined for literary distinction…. Niles will be the next cult horror novelist. *Savage Membrane* proves that."

—**Chris Wyatt,** *Cinescape*

"Steve Niles has created a fascinating character in the course of just one novel, and a frightening world that could produce many more interesting cases for Cal McDonald…. A great and involving read."

—**Terence Nuzum,** *Pop Culture Review*

"Cal McDonald's world is a terrifying place where anything bad that can happen probably will. Anyone who has read Niles's comic work in *Fused* and *30 Days of Night* knows he's a gifted writer. *Savage Membrane* proves definitely that his skills as a novelist are equally strong."—**Alan David Doane,** *Simply Comics*

HORROR AND DARK FANTASY
Published by ibooks, inc.:

CAL McDONALD MYSTERIES
by Steve Niles
Savage Membrane
Guns, Drugs, and Monsters
[coming October 2005]

THE J. MICHAEL STRACZYNSKI COLLECTION
Demon Night • *Straczynski Unplugged*
Othersyde • *Tribulations*

THE ROBERT BLOCH COLLECTION
Psycho • *Psycho II* • *Psycho House*
American Gothic

Sineater
by Elizabeth Massie

Werewolf
by Peter Rubie

SAVAGE
MEMBRANE

CAL McDONALD, MONSTER HUNTER
Book 1

STEVE NILES

ibooks
new york
www.ibooks.net

DISTRIBUTED BY SIMON & SCHUSTER, INC.

A Publication of ibooks, inc.

Copyright © 2002 Steve Niles

An ibooks, inc. Book

This is a work of fiction. All characters and events
in this book are fictitious. Any resemblance to persons
living or dead is strictly coincidental.

All rights reserved, including the right to reproduce this book
or portions thereof in any form whatsoever.

Distributed by Simon & Schuster, Inc.
1230 Avenue of the Americas, New York, NY 10020

ibooks, inc.
24 West 25th Street
New York, NY 10010

The ibooks World Wide Web Site Address is:
www.ibooks.net

ISBN 1-4165-0409-5
First ibooks, inc. printing February 2005
10 9 8 7 6 5 4 3 2 1

Cover art copyright © 2004 by Breehn Burns
Cover design by Brandon Diaz

Printed in the U.S.A.

To Nikki,
My Favorite Monster

ACKNOWLEDGMENTS

Special thanks to the following:

Ted Adams, John Lawrence, Breehn Burns,
Brian Holgiun, Beau Smith, Robbie Robbins,
Kris (the slasher!) Oprisko, Terry Fitzgerald,
Mason Novick, Clive Barker, Jon Snider,
Don Murphy, Brad Gould, Brent Ashe, Emek,
Paul Lee, Mark, Dante and Geoff,
Ann Chervinsky, and my entire family.

Without their help, support and friendship,
this book would not have been possible.

1

It was the night after Halloween. I had vague memories of crashing a costume party with a couple of ghouls I know. I started drinking. After that I draw a blank, but I'm sure there was trouble—there always is. Besides, I could feel a hell of a fat lip throbbing and my hands were cut and bruised with the unmistakable indentations of human teeth across my knuckles. I'd hit somebody and somebody had hit back. That didn't bother me so much. I was always hitting and getting hit. What I found disturbing was my empty shoulder holster. My .38 was gone.

I was face down in my apartment, experimenting with the adhesive properties of vomit and hardwood floors, when, of course, the phone rang. It sounded like a hammer against a steel barrel inside my skull. I groaned and peeled my face from the floorboards. My stomach lurched. It didn't like the idea of being moved very much but the phone was ringing incessantly. It was six at night so I had to get up anyway, but I didn't like being nagged. Wiping my face with one hand, I snatched the receiver violently from the cradle, choking the brain-rattling ring in half.

"McDonald Investigations. What d'you want?" I barked. My voice was gravel and phlegm.

The voice on the other end blurted, "Cal. I got something down here you might want to see."

It was Blout. Jefferson Blout is a big, bad ass cop from the precinct I worked in for all of a year. That is, before I was asked to leave as a result of a drug test. Evidently traces of alcohol, marijuana, and crank were found in my blood. Traces, hell! At that time I was practically sweating the stuff. They didn't need to check my blood, they could've just sucked on my arm.

Blout stuck by me when everyone else on the force had turned their backs. He knew why I did all the drugs, and why I still do sometimes. He knows what these eyes see. Christ. Believe me, if every time you turned around some fucked-up monster was coming down on you, you'd stay wasted too.

You see, I have this knack. Call it power, talent, what you like. I call it a curse. A fucking pain-in-the-ass.

It's like this: Some people attract love or money, and some—I think I'm one of the few—attract the bizarre. Always have, ever since I was an eight-year-

2

old kid living in the 'burbs. That's when I found my first corpse.

I'd been tooling around the woods, playing with sticks and crap, when I came over an embankment near the creek that ran parallel with my house. There it was, tucked in the mud and leaves like a big, naked peapod. I saw its feet first, then the torso. And that was all, because that's all there was. It was headless.

Maybe that was when things clicked, when my fate was set in stone. I wasn't scared, though—more like enthralled, so much so that I didn't bother to call the cops for over an hour. All I could do was think about the headless man. Who was he? Who killed him? And why had they taken his head?

Somehow, I knew instinctively that the head wasn't in the area, and when the cops arrived I told them my theory. They laughed, patted me on the head, and said I'd make a great detective.

That pretty much set the tone for the rest of my life: bizarre crimes, laughing cops, and me in the middle. Like I said, I'm a magnet for the weird, so I did what the cops told me all those years ago and became a detective. Now I really get on their nerves.

Anyway, Blout's supported me, helping with cases and sometimes with bail. I've tried to return the favor whenever something strange comes along that normal police investigations and procedures can't touch. And believe me, they hate to admit when they need help—especially from the likes of me.

There was this case a few years back where body parts of young boys and girls were being found all over the place—tragic, but not altogether uncommon. What was odd was that the limbs and other body parts hadn't been crudely chopped off, the norm in a hack-and-slash case. Instead, they were removed with almost perfect surgical precision. The killer took his time with these kids, lots of time. Even weirder, the parts were rubbed with strange oils and exotic herbs. The cops waited almost six months before they came to me. If not for Blout's insistence, they may never have.

Once they showed me everything, I knew immediately that we were dealing with something of voodoo origin. The herbs and oils were commonplace in Haiti and New Orleans, even certain parts of New York. But the surgical accuracy behind the removal of the limbs had me stumped until a day or so later. I was walking through an alley on the way to the corner liquor store, when I spotted an illegal chop shop—a garage where stolen cars are cut up for parts. It hit me like a ton of bricks, or better, a ton of bloody body parts.

I suggested the cops check the Feds' files for plastic or transplant surgeons of Haitian descent from the New Orleans area that had been fired in the past five years and had relocated to the Washington DC Metropolitan area. Second—and this even creeped me out—hit the files for stalking investigations on the Internet, specifically cases involving adults seeking teenagers.

On a hunch, I told them to check out a guy I'd seen on the news, name of Francis Lazar. He headed an organization that actually believed young children, and I mean young, were capable of physical relationships with adult men. The organization was called ManChildLove. I remember when I saw Lazar on CNN I quickly lost track of what he was talking about and concentrated on his eyes. In them I saw mania. The guy was a sick, twisted freak hiding behind his rhetoric.

Bottom line, boys: keep your eyes peeled for one or two twisted fucks with a penchant for teens, home surgery and voodoo.

Sure enough, everything I told them involving the case fell into place. The cops, with the help of the Feds (who love to come in right at the end), located one Dr. Polynice, formally of New Orleans and fired from his post for "unusual practices with cadavers."

In his basement, the authorities discovered the good doctor's very own teenage chop shop and Voodoo Lounge. After checking phone and mail records, it was found that the doctor had been shipping large crates all over the States. Before each shipment, a call was made from the Doctor to MCL spokesman Francis Lazar.

Connection made, target hit. Bull's-eye. Dr. Polynice's network was collecting innocent teenagers, murdering them, rearranging their body parts into unidentifiable corpses, and reanimating the patchwork cadavers with forgotten voodoo zombie rituals. And it gets worse, if that's possible. The bastards were selling the jigsaw kiddies to ManChildLove members. What those twisted pricks did with them I'll leave to your imagination.

It took me less then a week to solve the case after the cops had jerked around for six months because they couldn't stretch beyond their own perception of the world. How many kids could've been saved if they'd called me sooner? That's the question I couldn't shake.

In the end, more than sixty people were arrested from DC to San Diego and charged with crimes ranging from murder to kidnapping to necrophilia. Arrested were members of MCL, lonely, disturbed women and one or two well meaning but extremely misguided couples unable to adopt or procreate.

Throughout the trial, the subject of reanimation was never brought up, nor were the zombie teens ever shown, talked about, or presented as evidence. They just disappeared, victims for all time. Nobody wants to believe in Frankenstein, but they will believe that someone mail-ordered corpses for sex.

Soon as I heard Blout on the phone this time, I knew something strange was happening. Something the cops couldn't handle using conventional methods.

"What is it? Emergency? 'Cause if it ain't, I got a lot of throwing up to do."

Blout laughed. "Yeah, I heard about last night."

I didn't want to let on I had no idea what happened at the Halloween party, so I returned the laugh and said, "It was a great party. I had a good time." I laughed again. It was one chuckle too many.

"You have no idea what happened last night, do you?"

I paused as long as I could. "No."

There was an awkward silence that happens every time Blout and I come too close to personal talk. He went on.

"You going to come down here or not?!"

I belched. Bile boiled in my throat. "Yeah, yeah, give me a couple minutes to clean up."

"Please do."

He hung up before I could retort. Bastard.

2

I took off my filthy clothes and used them to wipe up the area where I slept, then threw them out the window into the alley. It would be easier to get new stuff than to pay to have vomit, blood and God knows what else cleaned out of them. I drew all the shades, lit a smoke and strutted around the apartment naked until I found myself standing in front of my half shattered, full-length mirror. It'd been a long time since I'd looked at myself. What a mess; a maze of scars covered my body. I looked like a scarification fanatic, except they do it on purpose. I got mine quite unwillingly, the result of years and years of getting the shit kicked out of me.

I shook my head. Only thirty years old but you'd think I was in my late forties. Christ, fifties even! Standing there naked, I realized I looked as much like a monster as any I'd fought. I laughed a breathy, gasping-for-air laugh. Yeah, fucking hysterical.

I turned towards my trash-covered desk, head pounding. My guts were twisting so I pulled open the bottom drawer where a bottle of Jim Beam greeted me. It went down hard and connected with the craving in my bloodstream, making me queasy. The sick retreated before I returned the bottle to the drawer. Hair of the dog wins another in a long series of battles.

Kicking a trail through ankle deep trash, I made my way to the bathroom, figuring I could catch a quick shower and shave and get down to the station within a half hour.

Just then I heard a sound from the other side of the shower curtain. Someone (or something) had shifted. I reached for my gun, but all I got was a handful of armpit. I had no weapon and I was naked, so I began to ease out of the room.

The curtain flew open and I screamed. A huge, dark figure stood in my tub.

"Ahhhhh!"

"Hey Cal, when did you wake up?"

It was Mo'Lock; sometime partner, reluctant friend, full-time ghoul. A ghoul of the lurking variety. My heart was pounding so hard I thought for sure I would die right then and there.

Yeah, I see all sorts of shit. Ghouls are actually one of the more common monsters around. They can be found all over the world, mostly in urban areas. They are the purest form of the undead, and actually the most harmless. Way back in the Middle Ages, ghouls were known for eating flesh and lurking in graveyards, but they came into their own around the turn of the century when they realized they didn't need flesh or blood to survive.

While the world was living through an industrial revolution, ghouls began a revolution of self-discovery. They were dead, cursed to live forever in a twisted form of their former human self, but they didn't need anything to survive. They made peace with the human race and began a hundred-year process of acclimating themselves into human society.

These days you can find ghouls everywhere. They tend to favor service industry jobs because they like the hours. Next time you pass a road crew, take a second look. I guarantee there's a ghoul among them. The same goes for postal workers and a wide range of people you probably never look at twice. Most people would be surprised how often they're in contact with the dead. All in all, ghouls are pretty low maintenance—that makes them all right in my book.

I met Mo'Lock on one of my earliest cases and he's been glued to me since. He has an annoying habit of creeping around, but I can't get too mad. That would be like blaming a cat for being hairy.

A slit of a grin appeared on his stark white, bony

face. "You forgot I was here, didn't you?" He looked a little too pleased with himself.

I took a deep breath. "Get the hell out of my bathroom. I got a call from Blout. Something's up."

The ghoul stepped out of the tub with long, sweeping, puppet-like motions. Two strides and he was standing outside the bathroom facing me. He looked me up and down like a ten-cent peepshow.

"Do you know you're naked?" He seemed to be genuinely concerned.

I slammed the door in his face. It hit him, and he fell to the floor cursing. He was very tall and thin, like a bone rail. Getting himself off the ground was a major pain. Teach his dead ass to mess with me. Maybe it would be a good day after all.

I showered, shat, shaved and dressed before returning to my desk, where the ghoul was emptying his pockets onto the blotter: mace, a lock-blade knife, handcuffs, and a pair of short spiked steel knuckles —an inexpensive, but nasty cousin of the brass knuckle—covered the stained desktop.

"Hey, don't go dumping your shit on my desk!"

"This is your 'shit.' I took it from you at the party after your episode with the alien," he said, "Besides, I do not have any 'shit.'"

He wanted me to see the bloody smashed mess the

door had made of his nose, but I just stared at him. His busted nose wasn't any big deal, it'd heal before we got to the precinct. The undead have amazing healing capabilities. He just wanted some easy sympathy.

"Officer Blout called again while you were in the shower. I took a message," Mo'Lock said as he lifted a piece of paper off the desk. "He said, 'If you don't get your fat, lazy-fuck, bastard-self down to the station immediately, you can kiss my black ass.'"

I loaded the stuff Mo'Lock had been holding for me into my pockets. Six-thirty P.M. and I was ready to start my day. When I headed for the door, Mo'Lock lumbered behind me. I stopped.

"You coming?"

"Do you mind?"

"No, not at all. You got cash?"

"Yes."

"Let's grab a cab."

The ride to the station was the usual bit of the bizarre that I've come to expect. The driver was of Mo'Lock's ilk, and the two of them gabbed on and on in a tongue that sounded foreign, but was simply regular English spoken at unbelievable speed. It's fascinating for about thirty seconds, then it works your nerves to blunt nubs. Moments like these made me wonder what the hell I was doing riding in a cab with a couple of the living dead. It was the eternal question: why me?

3

As a rule, I detest police departments, but I really hate my old precinct. Aside from the stares and nasty comments thrown my way as I pass, the place has a smell that sets my memory reeling. Walking the halls, I'm always reminded of the worst times.

The year I graduated from the Academy, for instance, was a long, shit-pile of a year. I became a cop, then lost my family and nearly my mind. In the space of twelve months, my mother and younger sister were killed by a drunk driver and my father, Ben McDonald, went berserk and cut the driver's throat outside the courtroom. As usual, I couldn't do a damn thing about it because I was so loaded on smack.

My father was charged and he responded by hanging himself the night before his hearing. I discovered the body. I'll never forget the image of his corpse swinging back and forth, the sound of the rope creaking against the rafter beam, rhythmic and maddening.

All my life I tried my damnedest to be normal. I ignored the dark fringes of the world that crept toward me and if something got too close, I stomped it dead and turned my back like nothing had ever happened. Monsters? Nope, didn't see them. Werewolves, aliens, demons and freaks? Just keep on walking. Don't look.

The Police Academy was an attempt at normal existence, but even there I should have known it would be impossible. I could never hide or live a normal life. No matter how hard I try, I always seem to land right in the middle of Freak Central.

The Academy was no exception.

It turned out that the place was built on a goddamn burial ground. Of course, the dead decided to have their revenge the week I arrived. It was a bloodbath of possession, sacrifice and the living dead. I don't mean living dead like Mo'Lock, bloodless ghouls who can function and think; these sons-a-bitches were mindless, kill-crazy zombies.

The place turned upside down. Everyone panicked except me. The one benefit of my life is that I'm never surprised. I've had the crap scared out of me a few times, but I never panic. That day, I fought my way through the relentless invasion until I reached the little room used as the Parish. I convinced the priest, who I found hiding in his confessional, to follow me to the basement where I told him to bless the water main. It took some convincing, and a slap or two, but eventually he agreed.

It was in the bag. I manned one of those riot control hoses and hosed the place down with a half million gallons of high octane Holy Water. The dead and possessed withered and melted, screamed and let loose the innocent. In the end, only a few dozen were dead and nobody except me and the priest knew what happened. Well, at least that was the official stand. The Academy closed and moved to a new location a year later. Chickenshits.

Still, I refused to give in, to acknowledge the supernatural regions of life. To hide, I took more and more drugs, more and more drink, anything to blur my vision or dull my senses. It was a miracle I lived, let alone graduated. But I did, and everything was going great for awhile. I even made the effort and kicked drugs. It was hard, very hard, and not just because of my physical and emotional addictions. The more I stayed sober, the more horror I saw: strange things peering around corners, voices whispering in my ear in the dark. But I had to make an effort, had to make some sort of a stand against the darkness that threatened to overtake me.

I was absolutely straight the day of my graduation from the Academy. My family was there (it would be several weeks until the drunk driver entered our lives) and though nobody said outright, especially my dad, I knew they were proud.

At one point he caught me alone near a crowd of rowdy graduates. He shook my hand and in a very low tone said, "You look good, son. Nice job."

He used the pretense of the graduation to congratulate me on kicking drugs, but it was better than nothing. Then in the crowd I saw a stranger moving quickly through the crush. He moved with a confidence you don't see in a normal person. I couldn't take my eyes off him, even though my father was talking to me. He broke through the crowd, and as he passed he looked at me and raised his hand. Then I saw his palm and the strange scar burned into its center. A pentagram—the mark of the beast. I started to go after him, but stopped. I wasn't going to give in. The darkness would not consume me. I forced myself to look away. When I looked back, the stranger had disappeared into the throng of graduates.

The next night I had dinner with my parents. I stayed sober despite the sight of the man in the crowd. It had been eating at me all night, though, because he seemed to take pleasure in taunting me. I knew what the man really was—a pentagram on the palm was the sign of the werewolf.

The dinner was nice despite my preoccupation. They were happy about me becoming a police officer and my newfound sobriety. Nobody said it in so many words, or any words at all, but they buzzed around, smiling at nothing, and there was a general air of peace that had been absent for a long time. My little sister Stephie suckered me into playing Nintendo with her after dinner and we wound up playing for hours. Finally, after I'd received countless ass-kickings, my dad asked that we turn off the game so he could see the news. I pretended to be disappointed, but it was a relief.

Everything came crashing down when the television flickered to life. The lead story on the news was a gruesome, extremely bloody multiple murder. To our horror, we found out the murders had happened nearby. A family was having a small party celebrating their daughter's graduation from the Academy. Details were sparse, but at some point the party came under attack—twelve people were slaughtered.

My stomach began to tighten. I needed a drink, a pill, something. Anything to stop the feeling rushing over me.

"...details are sketchy but police are telling us that this shocking tragedy seems to be result of some sort of... animal attack."

I was numb, sick. I felt responsible for the deaths. I had the killer in my sights and let him go.

I suddenly felt panicked and had to get out of that house. I hastily thanked my mom for the dinner as the whole family pleaded that I stay. I remember looking back as I got into my car and seeing my parents standing in the doorway. They weren't waving. They just stood there watching me, knowing I was about to leap off the wagon. They were right—I went on a binge that would've shamed Keith Richards.

It did the trick. I felt nothing but the buzz of alcohol and painkillers in my system. Above all, I saw nothing.

Three weeks later, a drunk driver took my family. After that, and after I found my dad swinging by his throat, I was gone. I remember nothing from the last half of my year as a cop save for loads of crushing pain. It was then that I faced my fate, spit on it and kicked it in the balls.

I was so much of a mess that my sergeant demanded I take a drug test. The results were bad. They didn't just ask me to leave the force, they kicked my butt and threw me bodily from the station.

It was the final straw. Still, I didn't care. I laid in the gutter until I had the strength to stagger to a liquor store. I was beaten down, twitchy and paranoid. Faces stared, some dumbly, some seemingly loaded with malice. I had lost it all. Soon I would come apart at the seams, or if I was lucky, just collapse and die.

Then it happened. I was walking, swigging rotgut, alongside a small shadowy park off Fifteenth Street, just short of Mount Pleasant. It was a dark moonless night, yet when I glared into the park I could see clear as day. I saw the figure of a man looming over a woman. At first I thought they were making out, and I began to turn away to get back to feeling sorry for myself. Then I saw the moist glimmer of fangs.

Vampire.

I tossed the bottle, smiled and cracked my knuckles.

I ran into that park feeling every ounce of the pain in my chest, every loss I'd suffered and most of all, the hatred I felt for the horrible luck I had. I channeled the rage into my body, feeling strong, sober and clear-headed. In reality, I was out of control, drunk and over-confident.

I attacked the vampire with such ferocity that the bloodsucker seemed frightened and tried to get away. From me, a mere human! In that moment, I gave up trying to run away. If the dark wanted me, it had me.

I ripped the head from the vampire's shoulders with my bare hands, pissing on the fate that was handed to me. This was my life. I had arrived.

And that, to make a short story long, is why I hate going to the precinct. It reminds me of my family and the sorry state of my life.

Blout was waiting for us outside the door of the coroner's lab, chewing on a big sloppy cigar. Normally I dislike cigar smokers, but he pulled it off. Blout was a large, wide-framed black man in his early forties, very dark and tall. In fact, he was almost as tall as Mo'Lock. He always wore dark suits that made him all the more imposing, making me feel small and unimportant in his shadow.

He looked pissed—pretty much his natural state—and none too pleased that I brought the ghoul along. Nobody could quite figure out who or what Mo'Lock was. He definitely made humans uneasy, but he always wore a suit and tie, so they assumed he was okay. Funny what you can pull off with a decent suit.

Blout stood up and looked straight into my eyes. Mo'Lock was ignored with clear, obvious disdain.

"What'd you bring him for?" Blout asked in his low, rumbling voice. He stood close. I could smell the minty stink of his menthol shaving cream and the fast food taco he had for lunch.

I shrugged. "He's my assistant. Might be able to help."

Blout shoved a big finger close to my nose. "Just keep him the fuck away from me. Got it?"

I showed him two palms. "Okay, no sweat. What've you got?"

Blout bobbed his head sideways, indicating the door of the coroner's lab.
"In here."

The lab was cramped, bare of equipment, and dark. There were only two lights; a small desk lamp and a bare bulb dangling above the examination table in the center of the room.

There was a body on the table, head and chest cut open. The scalp had been sliced, and the flesh from the top of the head peeled like an orange. The face of the dead man was wrinkled and folded down over itself. It would have been comical if it weren't so disgusting. The ribs were sawed clean away so there was a tidy viewing window to examine the cavity. I could see the internal organs had already been removed for examination. The heart and liver were in steel trays and next to them was an array of bloody saws and surgical tools. An autopsy had recently been completed.

I stepped up to the table. The body was male. By

the looks of his overgrown hair and the haggard, leathery look of his skin, I assumed he was homeless. That is, of course, when he was alive. He was dead now. Homeless and lifeless, what a raw deal.

Mo'Lock stayed behind me, close to the exit, but slowly edged toward the corner where there was the least amount of light. Blout moved to the other side of the table. He looked down at the body and sighed. He didn't have much of a stomach for an experienced cop. When he looked up at me I was screwing a cigarette into my mouth. His expression went from disgust to irritation.

"Don't smoke in here, Cal. Christ, you know better."

I put my lighter back, leaving the unlit cigarette in my mouth. "Yeah, I wouldn't want to give the stiff cancer," I said. "What's the story?"

"John Doe, homeless. He was found last night stuffed in a drainage pipe that used to dump into the old reservoir near the DC/Maryland border."

I could see no reason why I was needed. Dead bums weren't my forté, and not the least bit strange. I chewed on the unlit cigarette like a piece of beef jerky. "What's the cause of death?"

Blout smirked. He thought he had one on me, as though the answer were so clear, so obvious. "Try

24

opening your fucking eyes. You notice anything missing?"

I scanned the body again, stopping at the head. I leaned down and squinted into the open skull. Inside it was a clean white, as though the cavity had been scrubbed and bleached.

"I'll be damned," I said, and stood up straight.

"You see why I wanted you to come down."

From the other side of the room, Mo'Lock emerged from the shadows. "What is it?"

Blout and I spoke at the same time.

"No brain."

The autopsy was conclusive: the skull was completely empty. There was no blood, no matter, and x-rays showed there were no breaks in the skull whatsoever. The brain stem was there, untouched, as though there had never been anything attached to it. The official coroner's report called it brain death, but isn't brain death when you're still alive but a vegetable? How can something that isn't there be the cause of death? I'd like someone to explain that one.

The strange thing was, I'd seen this before. Blout knew it.

"Remind you of anything, Cal?"

I nodded. This time Blout kept his mouth shut.

Mo'Lock walked right up to the table. He stood so close I could feel the cold of his flesh, his annoyance evident. "Excuse me, but I'd like to know what's going on."

I was staring at the floor, my head swimming in watery visions of distant memories.

4

It was one of my earliest cases, during a phase when I was doing some pretty hard drugs. I was still a mess from what had happened with my family. It had been only a few months since I'd been thrown off the force, but I decided to go into business for myself—what did I have to lose? The way I figured, if weird shit was constantly getting in my face, I might as well get paid for it. I managed to throw together enough cash to get the apartment that I use as an office, and soon after began getting a few cases.

Most of them were simple, basic demon possession or hauntings. Other jobs were total fakes, people who thought their neighbors were Satan worshipers, vampires, and werewolves. Sometimes they were, but mostly they weren't. I didn't tell them that, though—I needed the cash. I had rent to pay and a bad habit to feed. Actually it was more difficult to cheat people than it was to deal with supernatural problems. I hated to lie, but cases involving the unnatural are pretty hard to find. It's tough making a living off something people refuse to believe exists. Things have to get way out of hand before they seek help.

That's what happened the day a guy named Edgar Cain developed a bizarre and dangerous ability. The police, at wit's end, were forced to turn to me.

Edgar lived in a huge, four-hundred-unit apartment complex. He was a lonely man, keeping to himself and hiding in his apartment for weeks on end. He was employed as an accountant for a company that did telemarketing and was thus able to work from home. It cut him off completely from contact with others, insuring his solitude. All that loneliness right smack dab in the middle of a tower of humanity was the catalyst for Cain's ability. Over the years I've found loneliness to be the source of many bizarre crimes and unnatural behavior.

One morning, residents of Cain's complex started to drop dead. Just like that. Bam, they're dead. By noon the body count reached seventy-five. And like the current stiff lying before me, their brains were gone. Not broken, splattered or spilled. Gone.

All the while, Edgar Cain grew inside his apartment. With each death, Cain's brain increased in size and so did his skull and head. Somehow, he was absorbing the brains of everyone around him. With the brains came their intellects, memories, and ideas. In his own horrific way, Edgar Cain undid years of loneliness by making a community inside his enormous, growing head.

That was the point where I came in: scores dead and a giant head going berserk on the top floor of an apartment building. The cops had come to the right guy—it had me written all over it.

Of course, I was wasted that day, but this time it would work in my favor. I didn't know it right away but Edgar couldn't absorb my brain because of the tremendous amounts of narcotics swimming in my blood stream. When I marched off the elevator with a shotgun, there was nothing he could do to stop me.

But I didn't just run in shooting. First I tried to reason with him. He ranted on about becoming one entity, one life, making loneliness impossible. Blah, blah, blah. After the speech, he attacked me and went airborne. The fucking head could fly! I tried to shoot him but only managed to blast his skinny little leg. He hit me hard. We went out the window, and just like that, we were flying over the city, a thousand feet up. I was clinging to his hair, ears, an open wound, anything to stay on while I punched and kicked at the wailing head.

Then I remembered the syringe in my pocket that I had shot up with earlier. I used that very syringe to stab out Cain's eyes and bring him crashing to the ground. He exploded in a massive spray of tissue and bone-chips, which conveniently broke my fall. A perfect ending—I was alive and there was nothing left of the head.

5

"End of case. Until this," I finished. I looked from Mo'Lock to Blout and then to the body. "I thought it was a simple case of spontaneous phenomenon, but if it's happened again..."

Blout shook his head, "What the hell's spontaneous phenomenon?"

"I made it up," I said, "It means something that's never happened before."

Blout raised his hands. "You can't make up case descriptions!"

"Sure can," I shot back, "I just did."

Blout was about to blow his top. The fact that I smiled didn't help.

"There has to be a source." Mo'Lock said, moving the conversation back on topic.

I rubbed my eyes. "Exactly."

Blout looked at Mo'Lock's pale flesh and deep sunken eyes. The ghoul bothered him in a way he'd never admit. To even entertain the thought of the walking dead would drive a normal person over the edge. For a cop like Blout, whose entire existence is grounded in fact, the truth would kill him.

Blout started to say something, but before he got it out, the door of the lab was knocked open by someone pushing a cart. It was a young woman with a serious face and hair pulled in a tight bun wearing a dark blue coroner's office windbreaker. On the cart was a bagged corpse, and behind it another.

"You Blout?" she demanded as much as asked. "On the John Doe case?"

Blout nodded quickly, flustered as a third and fourth cart were rolled in. "Yes to both questions," he said. "What the hell's going on?"

The woman handed him a clipboard. "We've been trying to reach you. Beat cops found a dumpster full of bodies alongside the water treatment plant near Georgetown. Sign please."

Blout grabbed his head and shot me a look. "All homeless?"

"Near as I can tell." She stopped for one quick moment as she caught a glimpse of Mo'Lock and was out the door.

In the hall, they had begun to line the walls with carts and bodies. There wasn't any room left in the lab.

* * *

Seconds turned into minutes at Dead Body Central. We all did a lot of head shaking, muttering and heavy sighing. Everywhere we looked was a cart and body-bag. The place was a cadaver parking lot. I waited for Blout to say something, but when at last he spoke, it was anti-climatic to say the least.

"I better get back to the office to start sorting this shit out." He eyed me sharply from across the table. "Got any ideas?"

"A few. I think the first thing I should do is get ahold of the Edgar Cain files. Can you get them for me?"

Blout shook his head. "Whoa, whoa, whoa! Don't go running off on one of your tangents. That was a nice story, but I need to investigate on planet earth first."

"Would it hurt you to humor me before it's too late just this one time?" I said and smacked his shoulder.

Blout muttered something under his breath, then, "Give me an hour."

"What about Cain's phone records?"

"Oh, come on, Cal. Why do you want phone records? You know what a bitch those are to get." Blout looked irritated.

"Just a hunch. I'll fill you in if anything pans out."

I turned to Mo'Lock. "One thing's for sure, if John

Doe was found outside a drainage pipe and this crowd was near the treatment plant, we got one place we have to check out."

The ghoul bobbed his head. "The sewers."

"Right. Grab some of your buddies and check it out."

"I'm on it."

Out of the corner of my eye, I saw Blout shudder as the ghoul left.

I chuckled.

"That freak gives me the creeps," Blout said with a little extra gravel in his throat.

"Be glad he's on our side. You'd cry like a baby if you knew what he was capable of," I said. "Besides, he's saved my ass more times than I care to admit, so in my book that makes him a lifetime pal."

"The two of you make a lovely couple. Let's get out of here. These stiffs got a meeting with the butcher."

Right on cue, the Medical Examiner came in with a couple of her assistants following like little bloodthirsty ducklings. I was halfway down the hall when Blout stopped and went back to the door.

"Wilson? Would you mind starting with the head examination first? I need to know what you find."

"Sure. It's your show."

Blout caught up with me as I was heading out the front door. "Hey Cal, want your gun back?"

I stopped outside, bit the inside of my lip and turned. Blout was grinning. My stomach sank. "You have my gun?"

He nodded slowly.

"You were at the party?"

"After the police were called in."

I threw my hands up in the air. Fuck it, I had no idea what I'd done. The jig was up. "Okay, you got me! What the hell happened?"

"First," he said reaching into his coat pocket, "here's your piece. Try to hang on to it."

I took the gun and put it into the empty holster. "Go on. I can see you're enjoying the shit out of this."

"Well, it seems you took it upon yourself to break some kind of world record for most drinks consumed in an hour—"

"Skip the embellishments."

"You got blind, piss-drunk, and seemed to forgot it was Halloween and you were at a costume party. Evidently, you spotted this dude in a real convincing alien costume and you... went... nuts." He rolled the last word off his tongue by touching it to his teeth, causing an irritating hiss.

"Did I hurt the guy?"

"Oh yeah."

"I didn't shoot him or anything, did I?"

Blout shook his head. "No, no. Luckily your buddies disarmed you while you were getting riled up. All you managed to do was smash a forty-gallon punchbowl over his head and beat him with a table leg. It wasn't pretty."

I slapped my hand over my eyes. "Is he pressing charges?"

"I'd be expecting a large lawsuit in the not too distant future."

I waved off the whole mess. "Fuck it. I don't care. I'll think of something."

I started down the front steps. The night air was breezy and the first hint of cold tickled the surface of my skin. Fall was in full swing.

"Let me know when you find Cain's case file, and about the autopsy results."

Before the door closed I heard Blout laughing, saying "I'm on it," in his best Mo'Lock impression. It was horrendous.

Walking back to my apartment, I snagged a pint of rotgut from the liquor store and swigged. The bottle was empty by the time I reached my building, and I was feeling fine. A little bleary, but better.

I reached for the door handle, but it wouldn't budge. I gave it another tug. Nothing. It was stuck.

"Goddammit."

After one last yank I leaned in and inspected the door closely. The space between door and frame was clogged with hardened opaque crud. Some punk had super-glued the door shut. I was about to curse everyone under thirty, when I suddenly stopped. There was a sharp noise over my shoulder—a click.

The small hairs on my arms stood on end. Instinctively, I dove sideways. At that exact moment, the door exploded in a hail of automatic gunfire. I hit the ground hard and rolled, but the barrage followed me like a swarm of angry bees. I rolled as fast as I could and jumped to my feet, diving for cover into the alley. Not fast enough: I felt the sting of a bullet graze my shoulder.

Then, as suddenly as it began, it was quiet again. I was laying in a pile of rancid garbage and pigeon shit, bleeding and trying to stay as still as possible while a car screeched away. When I ran to the curb a smoke cloud from the tires still hung in the air. I could see the car ahead and a figure hanging out the window, throwing away the gun. He was wearing a ski mask, no gloves, and wristbands. I reached for my revolver, but the shoulder wound tore wider and stopped me cold.

The street looked like the set of *The Hound of the Baskervilles*. Smoke was everywhere. I pushed through the haze towards the receding car until I found the gun lying in water and leaves. I don't know a hell of a lot about guns but I was pretty sure it was an Uzi. That in itself was scary enough. To top that off, painted along the side of the gun were the words, "Cal McDonald."

Venturing a guess, I'd say it was meant as a threat. Rank amateurs. That out-of-control hail of bullets could have just as easily hit me as not. Some warning. And writing my name on the weapon? That was just plain stupid.

Then I noticed the entire door to my building was gone, blown completely apart. At least I could get in now.

My shoulder was bleeding, but not bad. I'd be able to sew it up myself.

6

Blout sent Cain's file to my apartment by courier. No phone records, and the rest I already knew. The evidence list, though—that I found fascinating. Most of the stuff was pretty standard, but I was surprised to see that an accountant who worked out of his home owned no calculator, computer, fax, or answering machine. His life seemed oddly devoid of modern conveniences.

About ten minutes after the courier dropped by, Blout called with the preliminary autopsy results. The heads of the first three victims were empty and sparkling clean. I was sure the rest would turn out the same. What did surprise me was what Blout said next.

Some of the corpses had been dead for more than five months.

I was getting the unsettling feeling this case was going to be a bit more difficult than my usual day-to-day monster-in-the-closet case. As far as I knew, Cain was the only loon to suck brains telepathically, and that ability died when I killed him. This was something new, something bigger, and something much, much deadlier. I wasn't sure if that case had anything to do with this one, but it was all I had to work with. I needed to establish a timeline of Edgar Cain's activities the day he started absorbing people's brains.

"By the way," I said into the receiver as I reached for the bottle, "someone tried to turn me into a greasy smear outside my apartment earlier. I got the gun. Can I drop it off for dusting and ballistics?"

Blout sounded amused. "Any idea who it was?"

"Zip. All I saw was a dark '65 Mustang, speeding away with three people inside."

"Why don't you run down here in a little while? I'll run the weapon, and we can grab some food and talk about the case. Suits upstairs are nervous that the press might catch wind and turn the thing into a circus."

"Give me half an hour. I took a slug in the shoulder. I gotta stitch myself up." I took a big swig of Beam.

"Christ, Cal. Go to the fucking hospital!"

I swallowed. The burn felt great. "No. I've been there a thousand times this month. It's nothing. I'll take care of it."

"Fine," was all Blout had to say. He hung up.

I chuckled. "What a granny."

I removed my dress shirt and did some sewing.

* * *

By eleven o'clock that night, I'd polished off the bottle, popped some speed and was at the station with the gun. The precinct was quiet. The only two people in the front office were me and the desk sergeant, an old-timer named Potts. He plastered a fake welcome smile across his bored, withered face.

"I'm here to see Blout."

Potts made a face like bile had just shot the length of his throat, picked up the phone and paged Blout.

I was about to take a seat when the front doors banged open. Two uniforms came in, noisily hauling an unruly who looked to be drunk and disorderly. I knew one of the cops, Dan Stockton. He was a major prick, disliked by more people than just me. He was pissed because he was still in uniform while everybody else made detective or better, bitter because he knew he was a nasty fuck that everybody hated, but mostly because it was just his nature. He was what you'd call a bad egg.

Stockton let his partner take the prisoner, and stopped—facing me. He was way too close. I was torn between a short lecture on personal space and jamming the cartilage in his nose through his brain.

"Well, well, if it isn't Cal McDonald," he sneered.

"What the hell are you doing here? This is a police station, not a junkie detective station."

He stepped even closer. I stood my ground.

"I got plenty of business here, Stockton. And all of it's none of yours, so why don't you just back off," I growled, curling my mouth into a nasty scowl.

Stockton's eyes blinked and stuttered. I'd got him. He wasn't so sure I'd back down. I could tell he was searching for something snappy to say, but all he could muster was, "Why should I back off?"

"Because I have an aversion to halitosis," I shot back.

It was a dud. He didn't get it. Instead of being offended, he was confused.

"What?" he sputtered.

I sighed. "Bad breath." I was disappointed that the fire had puttered out.

But Stockton snapped and went for his baton screaming "Motherfucker!"

I backed away fast and threw my bag down. If I was gonna fight a cop in the damn precinct, I didn't want to have a loaded Uzi on me. They'd just love that.

Stockton had his nightstick at the ready, violence flaring in his eyes. He could beat the crap out of me and get away with it. He was a cop, after all! If I fought back, he could slap me with charges and a free beating. I didn't give a shit. I had every intention of mopping the joint with the nasty little prick's face.

Before any blows could be exchanged, Blout came out of a side door. "Stockton, what the hell are you doing?!"

In the end, I was relieved there weren't going to be any punches thrown. I would have come out on the losing end of that particular stick any way you looked at it. Cops don't look kindly on flatfoots beating on uniforms in the hall of the precinct.

"Get the hell out of here," Blout spat.

Stockton gave me a nasty look and promptly left. It wasn't over. Blout was looking at me, pissed again.

"Do you think you could stay out of trouble for two seconds?"

I shrugged. "I'm willing to try," I said, picking the bag off the seat. "Here's the Uzi someone tried to kill me with."

Blout laughed a jerky, breathy laugh.

We left the Uzi with the lab to dust for prints and run ballistics, and left the precinct at around eleven-thirty. Blout was hungry, but I had other plans.

7

By midnight we arrived at the deserted apartment complex where Edgar Cain had lived. The place couldn't have been creepier. The streetlights were dead, but it didn't matter since four looming high rises would block out any moonlight. The way the buildings were laid out gave the impression that the architect had simply thrown blocks into the air, and the way they landed was how the apartments were built. It was planned chaos that created shadowy corners, blind spots, and black canyons even the bravest thug would be wise to avoid.

The complex was called Whitney Green. In some ways it could be compared to the gigantic, soulless projects in New York and Chicago, with two major differences. It was condemned, for one. But what made it ominous was when you looked around Whitney, you saw nothing. No graffiti, no gang signs. No homeless, no squatters. Not so much as a broken window since the day Cain slaughtered the tenants with his mind. The compound imprisoned the troubled memories of over a hundred dead.

Nobody, not even the lowest of lows, dared penetrate its boundaries for shelter. It was truly a haunted place.

Blout was not at all pleased to be there.

"This is ridiculous, Cal. There's nothing here!"

We each had a flashlight. I flashed mine forward into the pitch-dark courtyard leading to unit number four, Cain's building. My footfalls echoed around our ears. Behind me, Blout's breath was heavy and labored.

"I have to make sure. I got a feeling something's here. Something that can help us." I said, and started walking away from Blout. "I'm going in. You can stay here if you want."

Blout didn't need to think it over. "Just wait up, goddammit."

The flashlight did little to light our path once we were inside the building. The darkness had a texture like smoky tar that seemed to fight the light, only allowing it to penetrate a few yards ahead of us. I was looking for the staircase.

"This is crazy. Why don't we come back during the day?" Blout whined behind me.

My light landed on an exit sign above a red steel door. "Because you can find things at night that aren't there during the day."

"Listen to yourself, McDonald. You're nuts!"

I ignored him. Some people need to whine when they're frightened. I know I do. "This way," I said, guiding him to the red door as I gave it a shove.

Inside the stairwell a gust of rotten air greeted us. An echo gave voluminous dimension to the corkscrew tower as we stepped inside. The door creaked shut slowly and closed with a small but definitive click. Blout swallowed. Like it or not, we were in.

"Which way?" he asked.

"Up," I said. "Cain's apartment. Top floor."

I took the first step. Then, above us, we heard a door slamming.

I jumped back. Blout threw himself against the exit door.

"W... what the fuck was that? Wind?" Blout hissed. I could hear the dry crack of his throat.

"Probably not. Come on."

Hearts pounding, we went up the first flight, then the second and third. By the fifth floor we were both calm.

Bang!

This time it came from below us. My eyes had adjusted somewhat and I could see that Blout was covered with sweat.

"You okay?" I whispered.

47

"No," Blout croaked. "You realize that in high rises like this, it isn't really the fourteenth floor. It's the thirteenth."

"Yes, I thought of that."

"Does that figure into your case?"

"Everything does." We had reached the eleventh floor. I stopped and pulled a flask out of my jacket, took two short swigs, and offered it to Blout.

He grabbed it, took one mini-swig, washed it around in his mouth and spit it out. "Christ, what is that crap?!"

"You heard of 'premium'? That's 'sale'." I took one more drink and then pushed on.

Cain's floor was as I'd left it years before—completely destroyed. The walls and ceiling were ripped away. Plaster and tile littered the place, forming piles of dusty white. At the far end of the hall I could feel a breeze coming through the hole we'd made when we went airborne. I could see the shattered wall and the dark blue, star-flecked sky that filled the vacant space.

Exactly halfway down the hall was another hole where Cain had smashed through from the inside of his apartment. That was where we stopped.

"This is it," I whispered and shot Blout a glance.

He was looking behind him and wasn't listening to a word I said. "Blout?"

He turned. "What?"

"In here. Cain's apartment."

The hole was large enough so that the two of us walked through side by side. For me, walking into the apartment brought a rush of memories. Because of the massive amounts of drugs I was on at the time not all of my memory is available for recall, but standing in this room where so much violence had taken place brought it all back to me.

Cain had first attacked me when I was still several floors away. His strange power pulled at my brain, but he couldn't take it. The pain was unbelievable, like nothing I'd experienced before, like fingernails grinding along the base of my brain. It made a migraine feel like pure pleasure. Cain pulled, pushed, tugged and squeezed my brain. I was so determined, or so wasted, that I kept moving until I was standing square in the doorway.

I had a shotgun trained on the floating head, but it wasn't afraid.

I remember that we spoke.

"Why won't you leave me alone?"

"You killed all those people."

"I didn't do it," he said. "Didn't really kill them.

Only absorbed their brains. They were unhappy, all of them. Leading empty, pointless lives…"

The floating head paused, and swayed. I shot off one of his legs, and he hardly noticed.

"…like everyone else." He went on, "I simply combined them into one big pointless life."

Then Cain stopped talking and attacked. The fight wasn't over until I stabbed his eyes out high above the city and sent him crashing to his death.

* * *

"Cain had no remorse," I said.

Blout was at the window shining his flashlight along the shattered frame. "What was that?"

I shook my head. "I remember Cain talking like he did the dead a favor by taking their brains."

"He was a homicidal maniac. You were expecting logic?" Blout said. Then, as though suddenly annoyed, he turned off his light and raised his arms. "Would you please tell me what I'm supposed to be looking for?"

"Not really sure. I just needed to come here… to feel it."

"Well, are you done feeling it yet?"

"Look, Blout, I don't knock your methods. Don't knock mine."

I was getting pissed. I turned off my flashlight and waved him over to my side of the room. "Let's take a break."

As we pulled up boxes and sat, I took out my pack of cigarettes and the flask. I swigged and handed it to Blout. Before drinking he held it up to the moonlight coming through the window.

"Checking for germs?"

"No, just seeing if there was any left." Blout said and this time took a big-ass mouthful and choked it down. *"Ahhhh ahh!* Damn, that's awful." He coughed, then took another pull.

I smiled, thinking how odd it was that the two of us tolerated each other. We couldn't have been more different. He was successful, together and completely on the up-and-up. And me? I was in as much, if not more, trouble than I was in my teens. What a pair we made.

"You know, you have a name that should be in a Frank Capra movie. *Jefferson Blout Goes To Washington*." I displayed the marquee in the air with my hands.

Blout laughed. "Yeah, Capra made a bunch of films about black cops."

I took a drink and swallowed hard. "Can I ask you a question?"

Blout just shrugged. The last mouthful was his.

"It's what, two, three o'clock in the morning. Doesn't it bother your wife that you don't come home?"

Blout looked away and sighed. "Jessica left me last month. So yes, I guess it did bother her."

"Shit, I'm sorry. I wouldn't have brought it up if—"

"It's all right. We were married a long time, a lot of good years. I don't have any regrets." He was fumbling in his coat. His hand came out holding two of those jumbo cigars he smokes. "Want one?"

I was about to agree when I had an idea. "I'll be right back."

I got up and darted to the right where there was a small efficiency kitchen. I opened the refrigerator and smiled. I love it when hunches pay off.

"What've you got there?" Blout asked at my back.

I turned and showed him. "I present to you, one six-pack of the finest ten-year-old Black Label for our consuming pleasure. Warm, of course."

I planted the six-pack on the floor between us, broke one from the ring and gave it to Blout in exchange for the cigar. When I popped open my beer, it foamed. I took that as a good sign.

Blout was staring at his can. "Is this safe?"

"Only one way to find out." I swigged and was

surprised to discover that it tasted as crappy and watery as a new Black Label.

Blout sipped, testing. Finding it normal, he swigged away.

"What about you, Cal? Why haven't you ever settled down? I've seen you with some young women that weren't completely out of their minds."

"Thanks," I laughed. "The way shit comes flying at me, it's impossible. Nobody can take a life like that, and I wouldn't wish it on them."

"Come on. You're exaggerating. It can't be that bad."

I looked him square in the eyes. "My best friend is a fucking ghoul. It's that bad."

Blout stared at me for a full minute before he spoke. His voice lowered. It was serious time. "It really boggles me that you buy into all this crap."

"When a brick lands on your head, you start believing in bricks or you get your skull bashed in." I paused, feeling a speech coming on. "Don't you see, Blout, nothing is true if you don't believe, but if you do believe, really believe, you can create the impossible. The power of belief—*Braaappp!*—is a potent force."

Blout opened his second can and tossed me one, but I was already on my third. "Then explain this.

How come you're the only one who ever sees all this spooky bullshit? Can you tell me that? I never see any of it."

"It's right there in front of you. You just don't accept it. I see it because I believe. Ain't it the shit?" I stopped and gave a smirk. "But mostly because you're not looking. You've seen it. I've seen you see it."

"Bullshit."

I looked around at nothing in particular. "Maybe, maybe not. Ignorance is bliss, right?"

I stood. This conversation could only turn ugly. It was time to get back to work. I looked around the room. My eyes were more or less adjusted to the cool light of the moon. I could make out the corners and some muddied colors.

Blout stood as well. "So what aren't I looking for now? I know you're after something here."

"I'm trying to figure out where it began. Where was Cain when people started to die?"

Blout perked up. I'd finally given him something to work with. "In the report it said that the deaths started early, before noon."

I snapped my fingers. "The bed."

It was in the farthest corner from the front door, away from the window. The bed itself was crushed.

54

"It started in the morning. Cain started absorbing early and grew until the bed couldn't support the weight."

Blout had moved to the foot of the crushed bed, where he stood pushing debris away with his feet. "What do you make of this?"

I stepped to the end of the bed where Blout was looking down at the floor. There was a pentagram carved into the floorboards. I flashed my light on it as Blout kicked away more of the plaster and dust. Carved around it, smaller but no less prominent, were several other symbols: a Star of David, a pyramid, a cross and several that were so badly carved I couldn't venture a guess.

"Well?" Blout said. "How does this fit into your conductor theory?"

I shrugged. "It doesn't, but it doesn't discount it either," I replied, lamely trying to cover my ass. "It just means Cain wasn't getting his security deposit back"

Blout didn't laugh. "I'm outta here," he said and headed for the exit hole.

"Blout, wait. Just one more thing."

I got his attention. He stopped and turned. "One more?"

"One more, then we get breakfast."

"What is it?"

"I want to check out the basement."

"See ya."

I chased Blout halfway down the stairwell. He finally stopped on the ninth floor, not because I was pleading with him to stay and help, but because we were both horribly out of breath.

"You ask too much, Cal."

"I know, but you want to solve this thing, right? You've got a morgue full of people who died under very strange circumstances. It stands to reason that the solution is going to be as strange as the crime."

Blout laughed. "You're the only person I've ever met that talks in circles and comes out makin' sense."

"Basement, then breakfast?"

"Deal."

We started back down the stairs to check out the basement, but somebody had other plans. All at once, above and below us, the sounds of doors opening and slamming filled the stairwell.

Slam!

"What the hell is that?!" Blout yelled. The sound was deafening.

Slam! Slam!

We both had our guns drawn, cocked and waving at darkness.

Slam! Slam! Slam!

"Screw the basement!" I screamed. "Let's break for the first floor and get out of here!"

We got nowhere. I heard a rasping sound, and stink passed beneath my nostrils, making me gag. Then a board hit me flat on the back of the head and I went down hard, feeling my neck doused with hot blood. The hall was filled with attacking bodies. Blout was yelling and firing off rounds, but I couldn't do anything to help him. I was being beaten on every inch of my body.

There were so many attackers I couldn't breathe. When I gasped for air, all I got was a lung full of dusty, death-like stink.

I fell, gagging and trying to go limp, but there were a dozen fists and two dozen kicking legs waiting to meet me. It was too dark in the stairwell to see our attackers, and I was being hit too much to focus. The last thing I remember was hearing Blout screaming my name. As I began to lose consciousness, I reached out for support, but instead my right hand fell upon what could only be a face. I scratched where the eyes should have been but my fingers found nothing but dry empty sockets.

Then, mercifully, everything went black.

8

I was out cold, drifting in a state that would have been pleasant had it not been forcibly induced by a beating. I had a vague awareness of being dragged, surrounded by loud static noises, heat, flame and smoke. Voices barked and grunted, and as time passed I felt the presence of fresh air. Then more screaming and a sound that could have been the pounding of feet on concrete.

It all ended with a jolting blast of pain erupting in the back of my skull. I woke to the sights and sounds of the chaos I had been distantly experiencing while unconscious. It wasn't what I expected.

I saw daylight, early morning daylight. I was on my back, lying in the parking lot of Whitney Green surrounded by emergency medical personnel. They were looking down at me, poking and prodding my body, and talking like I was an idiot. I tried to sit up, coughing, pushing them away. Every millimeter of my person hurt. I felt broken ribs, a multitude of bruises and a gaping gash on the back of my head.

"Get off me!" I yelled at the medics, and stood with

great effort. It was then that I saw what had happened.

Cain's apartment building was an inferno. From the ground floor to the roof, fire tore away the structure. Flames shot from every window. Smoke billowed thick into the clouds overhead. Stopping the blaze was useless. The best bet was to contain it, and judging from the lackadaisical efforts of the firefighters, I guessed that was the plan.

Let it burn, let the haunted halls crumble. I'm sure that was what everyone was thinking. Erase the horror once and for all. I could see it in the eyes of the onlookers—they were watching a monster die.

I shook my attention away from the fire. I had to find Blout so I headed toward the nearest squad car where I found some medics working on a nasty swelling beneath his left eye. When he saw me, his eyes went wide. I had a pretty good idea what a bloody mess I was.

"Jesus H. Christ, Cal! Are you okay? My God, they really worked you over!"

"It's a karma thing, no doubt." I touched the back of my head. My hand came back soaked with sticky red. "Can I get a goddamn bandage here?!"

I finally allowed a pesky medic to bandage me up. They wrapped my ribs and put in a couple of butterfly stitches, including a few in the bullet graze that I'd stitched earlier. They doused each wound with antibiotics, which hurt worse than the damn beating, then finally backed off.

Meanwhile, Blout gave a very abbreviated report to his captain.

"...there was every reason to believe we had a connection between the bodies discovered early yesterday and the events that took place here ten years ago. We decided to check it out, but instead came across a bunch of crackheads. They attacked us, and I guess that's who set the fire."

Luckily, the Captain was too concerned with the arriving TV crews to notice the huge holes in the story. He wasn't even looking at Blout during the last half of the spiel.

"Um, okay... I want it on my desk by this afternoon," the Captain said, and was gone.

Blout rolled his eyes in my direction.

I winked, blew him a kiss and re-split my lip doing it. "Fuck!"

All I wanted to do was get back home. I needed to shower. I needed to sleep. But before that, I needed many drinks and smokes. Unfortunately, Blout wasn't finished. I tried to walk away from the rapidly burgeoning media circus when he came stomping up behind me.

"What the hell happened in there, Cal? How'd we get out? Did you do it?"

I kept on walking. "Last thing I remember was being in the stairwell getting the shit kicked outta me."

"Cal, stop. We'll take my car."

I fell behind him as we walked. He was asking too many questions too soon. My head was spinning and I guess his was as well. After all, he wasn't used to this kind of thing.

I caught up to him at the car. It was one of those bland blue jobs that looked like a giant matchbox car. "Is this thing for undercover?"

"Why?"

"Wouldn't fool a blind man. Why don't you just write 'COP' on the doors."

Blout wasn't amused. "I'll inform my superiors."

I got in. Blout stared ahead with a sleepy blank stare and then turned to me. "Any idea what we just got out of?"

"I'd bet that our attackers were also our saviors."

"What?! That makes no sense. What possible purpose would that serve?!"

"A warning, maybe," I said as the car jerked and rumbled to life, "possibly a diversion. All I know is those things could have offed us easily, and didn't. Hell, they could've just left us inside. But they did destroy the building. We were close to something, that's for sure."

We pulled out of the lot, waved on by a uniform guarding the exit, and drove for a while without saying a word. I sat there feeling every cut and bruise throb, and thought of morphine. I missed it, but I wouldn't fall into that trap again. I'd have to settle for some Percocet or something equally tame. Fuck.

9

After a large and much needed diner breakfast, Blout dumped me off at my place just short of noon. I felt bad for him—while I was planning to lapse into a painkiller-induced coma, he had to go back to the precinct and do paperwork.

Blout caught me looking at him as I pushed open the door. "I'll call you if anything happens," he said. "Get some sleep."

I slammed the door, then leaned down to the open window. "Let me know how the ballistics and crap turned out on that Uzi."

"Will do."

He pulled away with a screech and was gone.

As I turned toward my building, I noticed the door hadn't been fixed, just boarded up. It was a sloppy, erratic job with dozens of holes and jagged slits and it sure as hell wouldn't keep anybody out. Pull one nail and the whole job would fall apart.

Even worse, there was a little man in a suit waiting right beside the boarded door. He had a stained manila envelope tucked under his stubby arm. No doubt about it, he was here to serve me papers.

I thought briefly about running, but he'd seen me, and really, what would be the point? Sooner or later those little rat bastards manage to slip you the notice. So I just walked right up to him, stood a little too close, and stared down at him.

"A...are you Mr. Calvin McDonald?" The little weasel shook and broke a sweat.

I leaned in. "Yes."

As cowardly as the creep looked, he was quick. Without saying a word he crammed the envelope into my hands, scurried sideways and was walking away toward a hot little sports car when I heard him say without a shake in his voice, "You have been served."

I didn't open the envelope. I rolled it and shoved it into my back pocket, pulled the door open and went in. Everything hurt, as three flights of stairs painfully tugged, pulled and stretched each gash and bruise. And I don't mind telling you, I bitched and moaned every step of the way.

I stopped cold on the last step. My place was the first door on the left and I could see the door from where I stood. It was open. Just a crack, but open just the same. I took out my piece, planted my back against the wall and began edging along the flaking plaster until I was right beside the door. I held my breath so I could hear over my raspy, pained breathing. There was movement inside, drawers opening and closing, paper rustling. It didn't sound like a shakedown. They don't close drawers.

"Mo'Lock? Is that you?" I said low, almost a whisper. Ghouls have excellent hearing.

There was a second of complete silence. I lowered the gun at the crack in the door. Another second passed.

"Yes, it's me, Cal." The voice was Mo'Lock's unmistakable low rumble.

I jammed the gun back in my armpit and stepped through the door. The ghoul was at my desk, bent over, looking for something. He straightened and I saw that he was filthy, almost completely covered with grime and soot.

"Are you looking for a moist towelette?"

Mo'Lock bobbed his head. I'd confused him. Any sort of modern reference tends to throw off a guy who's been dead for over a hundred years. "Well," he said "something of that sort. I didn't want to muss up your cloth towels."

"Ah, go ahead. Just leave one for me."

That was all the ghoul needed to hear. He turned and trucked out of the room while I gingerly began removing my jacket and tie. Lastly, I kicked off my shoes and untucked my shirt and threw the envelope on the floor. I retrieved the bottle from the desk and several quick swigs later began to feel fuzzy and light. To add to the haze, I threw down a couple of painkillers. By the time the ghoul came back all clean and sparkly, I wasn't feeling a goddamn thing.

"So what happened? Did you find anything?"

Mo'Lock stepped up to the front of the desk and bent forward. "I assembled a couple of my friends as you asked—"

I interrupted him. "Please, for God's sake, sit down. You make me crazy."

The ghoul did as I asked, which brought him to just above eye level.

"My friends and I went to the drainage pipe where the first body was found. But first, I searched the area where the dumpster was located. We found an entrance to the sewer, but didn't go in. It was too small and smelled terrible. Instead, we doubled back to the larger drainage pipe and entered." He nodded at the end of the speech, as though some point had been made.

I shook my head. "And that's how you got dirty?"

"Let me finish."

"Sorry."

"After walking through the pipe for an hour, we came to an intersection. I believe it was somewhere below Dupont Circle." The ghoul spoke slowly and carefully, rolling out each word for maximum effect. Sometimes his speech patterns reminded me of a drunk trying to sound sober, but with an air of elegance that belonged only to the undead.

"Dupont? That's like five miles from the drainage pipe!"

"Yes, I'm aware of that. Anyway, that was where we found the hole."

I sat forward. "Hole?"

"Yes, and it was not city work, I can tell you. The pipe had been cut with a blow-torch and was very uneven, like the cutter started out trying for a circle, but settled for a square."

"Where'd it go?"

"For the first several yards it went east, maybe north-east."

I nodded. "Toward Whitney Green." I took another drink. My gums were numb and my scalp felt like it was swarming with ants.

"Possibly, but after those several feet the tunnel turned into an incline, and after that there was an unexpected drop... straight down."

I was getting a little impatient. At times he could be too efficient. "Did you go down?"

Mo'Lock looked away. "We had no choice... we slid."

I laughed. "And you got dumped into the pit!" I was feeling good.

I offered the bottle to the ghoul as peace offering. He waved it off. "No, thank you."

"Come on, it won't kill you," I urged.

He looked back toward me. "No, it won't kill me. It tastes bad."

The drink and drugs were making my thoughts wander. "When was the last time you ate or drank anything?"

He thought about it for a second. "Just a little over a hundred and ten years. Not counting the occasional mouthful of rainwater."

"Or a chunk of that guy's neck! Remember that?!" I was having fun. It was the best I felt all week. You gotta love painkillers.

Mo'Lock stuck out his tongue. "How could I forget? That tasted very bad."

We fell silent for a moment as Mo'Lock worked the memory of biting that guy through his mind. I lit a smoke. "So, you and your buddies fell in the pit..."

Mo'Lock looked up slowly. "It was a short fall into

another tunnel. We found that it went in two directions, so we split up. I went east by myself. The other two went west."

"What was the tunnel like?"

"Big, wide. I'd say twice the size of the drainage pipe," he answered, then continued. "I walked for a while. Didn't see much of anything. The tunnel was clean and quiet, like a spotless mining shaft. Very odd."

I laid my head on the desk.

"Then I started coming across exits. They were above me, and near as I could see they were normal manhole covers with these strange clamp locks welded to them. You know, like on preserve jars. There was one about every five hundred yards."

Tunnels and exits heading toward and away from Whitney Green. A web. Something solid was beginning to form, connections were being made. I just wasn't exactly sure where it all led.

Mo'Lock went on. "After another hour I began hearing noises ahead of me. I walked faster until I was running. The noises got louder as I got closer. At first it was just a banging sound, then voices."

I raised an eyebrow, but stayed head-down on the desk blotter.

"As I got closer to the voices and the banging, the

tunnel was no longer smooth. It was rough dirt with rocks, rats and trash everywhere. It was when I stopped running that I heard your voice."

That got my attention. I raised my head. "My voice. You heard my voice? Are you sure?"

"Yes, and Blout's as well. You were arguing. It was high above me and there was an echo."

I nodded for the ghoul to continue his story.

"I moved cautiously toward the sound of your voices when suddenly it changed to yelling and screaming. I thought you and Blout might be under attack so I ran, but unfortunately I was blocked by a large steel door. I pulled and kicked at it, but it was too strong. So I did all I could. I listened."

"Meanwhile, I was getting my ass kicked."

Mo'Lock ignored me. "A short time later a thunderous stampede came from the other side of the door. There was a great grinding noise, and then the door unlatched and flew open. I was face-to-face with your assailants. At first they didn't see me, but when they did, they started screaming and crying, cowering against the wall. They were terrified of me."

"What were they? Did you get a good look?"

"Undead of some sort. Nothing I'd ever seen before. They were mummified, dried skin tight against their skulls, with empty eye sockets."

I nodded. "That's them."

"I approached one that was near me. It screamed and carried on. I didn't mean to, but in trying to calm the thing, I accidentally grabbed a necklace that was around its neck, and it came off." Mo'Lock stopped talking and looked down at his feet. "It was terrible."

I didn't say a word. He'd go on when he was ready.

"The thing just turned into dust at first, but then it liquefied and became blood. Just like that, there was a pile of clothes soaked in blood." The ghoul shook his head. I guess it was a little too close to home for him.

"What happened next?" I urged.

"Chaos. The other things started running away, back the way I'd come.

I was about to give chase when I remembered you were somewhere on the other side of the door. As I started through, I was overcome by black smoke and intense heat. I tried to push on, but it was too much. I ran to one of the sewer covers. It was melted shut, so I had to break the concrete to escape. I could see the building on fire, but when I saw you and Mr. Blout were all right, I came back here."

"Did you say you broke the concrete?"

"Yes."

"With what?"

"My hands."

"You can break concrete with your hands?"

"If need be."

I smiled, recalling when I first met Mo'Lock. He was just your standard ghoul doing what ghouls do best: lurking in the shadows, wandering the earth soulless and aimless. He'd helped me out on a case because he thought I was a monster as well. He said it was a vibration I gave off. Sort of the supernatural equivalent of a butt sniff.

When I met him, he barely spoke. Now he could recount events as well as any detective I'd ever known. Better, really, with his heightened senses and all.

"What about your two partners and the necklace you nabbed?"

"I haven't seen them since. I'm a bit worried." He fumbled in his pocket and then held up an object. "This is what I pulled from the neck of your undead attacker."

He held up a simple homemade necklace. I took it from him. It was a plain strip of brown leather with a pendant attached, a small glass vial. Inside was what I took to be blood. That seemed to go along with the ghoul's description of what had happened.

"Amulet?" the ghoul asked.

I shook my head. "More like a talisman. Amulets

protect, ward off evil and things like that. Talismans make things happen."

I held it up to the light, turning it in my palm. No inscriptions or marks of any kind. Nothing that told me what it was, or where it originated. I had two facts; the object was a talisman, and the wearer had been a reanimated, mummified corpse. Its origins could range from Haitian voodoo priests to Egypt or South America. Every culture had some sort of reanimation ritual, but which one fit the tiny vial?

It was just another mysterious piece to the puzzle. I still had no clue what the big picture was.

I held the vial up to the bulb of my desk light again. I wasn't sure, but there seemed to be something else inside, floating in the blood. Probably a clot or a maggot.

I stared at the vial and shook my head. When I looked up to say something, Mo'Lock was gone. He was pinned against the wall, staring out the window—trying not to be seen from the outside.

"What is it?"

The ghoul turned to me. "Are you aware that someone is watching the apartment?"

"Dark colored sports car?"

"Yes. How did you know?"

"Lucky guess." I swallowed a huge mouthful of whiskey.

10

I told the ghoul to shut the blinds. I'd had enough for the week. Some downtime was needed or I was going to fall apart. The vial was stashed in a compartment inside the top drawer of my desk. It would be safe there until I wanted to deal with it. I took another Percocet, stood from the desk and zigzagged over to the couch. It was buried in trash. I cleared it off with a swipe of my aching arm, while Mo'Lock watched me curiously.

After I had the couch cleared, I opened the closet near the unused kitchen. I dug around in there until I found a small black and white television that I put on a chair in front of the couch.

Lastly, I went to the fridge and snagged a six-pack, grabbed the ashtray, whiskey, and smokes. Then I did something I hadn't done for years. I just sat my ass on the couch, turned on the idiot box and stared like a goon.

"*Ahhhhhhh,*" I moaned in relief. Each and every wound on my body purred and tingled. The painkiller was working its magic.

I immediately began to nod off. Mo'Lock shuffled his feet, bored. I suggested that he check out whoever was watching the apartment, and he was out the door.

Then the phone rang. I started to answer it, but decided to let the machine get it. After the tone I heard Blout's voice.

"Cal, are you there? Pick up."

I shook my head and yawned.

"Well, listen. The test on the Uzi came back. Whoever shot at you had no fingerprints. They were burned off. The rest of the test came back empty. They couldn't trace the weapon."

I started into the bedroom, but Blout went on.

"Another body matching the others was found. This time it wasn't some homeless guy. It was a history professor from George Washington University."

I ran over and picked up the phone. "I'm here! What kind of professor was he?"

"Like I said, history... uh, it says here something about folklore and myth. Sounds like he might be a friend of yours."

"Where was his body found? Sewers again? Because—"

"No, get this. The guy had been in a bad car accident about six months ago and lapsed into a coma—"

Lucky stiff, I thought.

"—and he stayed that way until this morning when he was found dead. When they cut him open, no gray matter, nothing."

I stretched and felt some of the butterflies tighten. I was close to passing out. "Look, Blout, we found dick in that apartment. Can you find out what happened to Cain's personal belongings? I noticed on the evidence list there were some books I'd like to take a look at." I yawned right into the receiver.

"Have you slept yet?"

"Nope."

"Neither have I. What say we check in with each other tomorrow?"

"Sounds good."

I dropped the phone into the cradle, turned, reeled into the closet I call my bedroom, and was out cold before I hit the mattress.

11

I woke up on the floor the next morning. I was groggy, but felt pretty good. It was Sunday, just before eleven A.M.—an eighteen-hour sleep. Eighteen hours of drug-induced, body-healing bliss. But soon enough my thoughts turned to the case. Something had been eating at me that I needed to check out.

Mo'Lock was waiting for me in the office. I had locked the apartment door and the front door and he had no key, but he still managed to get in somehow. I never asked how and he never offered the information. In the past, I would have been startled, but I was beginning to get used to it. It was just another ghoul thing, another of the seemingly endless talents acquired by those caught between life and death.

"Morning Mo'," I said, doing a beeline to the desk. I called Blout at the precinct. After a couple of holds and transfers, I got him on the line.

"Something's been bugging me," I said.

Blout didn't say anything, waiting for me to get on with it.

"Medical autopsies aren't usually performed on

John Does and homeless, are they? Why were they performed on the one we got?"

Blout wasn't impressed. "Well, the first one looked like he was thrown in the ditch. Possible homicide. The dumpster full I think you can figure out."

"But my point is, usually medical autopsies aren't performed on homeless found dead, are they?"

"Not if it looks clean," Blout said. "Dental records are checked for identification and then cause of death is determined. Most of the time there's no reason to open the chest, let alone the head."

"What about senior citizens who die of natural causes in retirement homes and hospitals?"

"Same. What are you getting at?" Blout sounded a little upset, possibly because he thought I was ahead of the game and holding out.

"What about people who die of a chronic illness—AIDS, cancer and the like?"

"There's no reason to do an autopsy. The cause of death is presumed known by the circumstances of the illness." Blout paused. "Look, are you going to tell me what this is about, or am I going to have to hang up?!"

"It's just that I think we should consider the fact that deaths like these could have been going on for awhile, months or even years. We just lucked out because whoever or whatever is behind this got sloppy." I was pleased with my coherent argument. "Is there any way we can get confirmation?"

Blout sighed hard. "I think you've got something there, but it would be next to impossible to find out. Usually John Does are cremated by independent funeral contractors. The rest could be anywhere. Besides, I can guarantee there's no way I'd get clearance to exhume any bodies."

I thought about that for a second. "I think it's enough that we consider the chance that this might have been going on for awhile. Maybe a very long while."

"I agree," Blout responded reluctantly. Maybe he was doing the math, like I had. The possible body count was daunting.

Blout went on. "Cain's personal belongings are stored in a warehouse next to the sixth precinct. I told them to expect you, so bring some I.D. and leave your freaky friend home."

"Thanks. Anything else?"

"No."

We hung up without good-byes.

The ghoul was standing by the window as usual. He was pulling up the shade I had asked him to close yesterday. Without looking my way, he spoke. "I tried to check out the subjects watching you, but when they saw me coming, they drove away."

"Did you get any kind of look at them?"

"There were three of them. They appeared to be fairly young, late teens, maybe early twenties. Two male, one female. What I found odd was that they all were wearing wristbands and scarves of some sort around their necks."

"Ascots?" I laughed. "No accounting for taste."

Mo'Lock's brow wrinkled as he squinted out the window. "Well, I'll be."

"What?"

"They're outside the apartment again." The ghoul said and looked my way. "One of them has a rifle."

"What the fuck are they doing?!" I started toward the ghoul and the window. Enough was enough.

Mo'Lock went on, "He's pointing it up here and—"

Blamm! Blamm! Blamm!

The window shattered and the ghoul's upper back exploded in three places. He flopped in the air like a marionette cut loose, then collapsed hard to the floor. I threw myself against the wall. Mo'Lock was spread eagle on the floor. No blood seeped from the three big holes in his shirt.

"You okay?" I reached out with my leg and gave him a little nudge with my foot.

"I'm fine," the ghoul said from the floor. "Don't kick me."

Nobody shoots my friends, even if shooting them doesn't hurt. I was pissed. I dove past the shattered window and grabbed my pistol off the desk. I was out the door before Mo'Lock could get to his feet. Taking the stairs by twos, I was outside in time to see the three fashion casualties getting into their Mustang. I wasted no time in raising the gun, and quickly squeezed off a few shots.

"Freeze, you sons-a-bitches!!"

My first shot shattered the back window of the car. The second and third went stray. The last three were anybody's guess. A thirty-eight caliber crap shoot.

The Mustang's rear tires spun. Burned rubber wafted across my face as I ran up to the curb, but the car was already gone, speeding away down the street and very nearly hitting a commuter bus. That would have been perfect, but they steered clear. For the second time, they had gotten away with shooting at me. But this time there was a silver lining. There was blood on the sidewalk. At least I'd hit one of the bastards.

It was then that I realized I was standing in the street holding a smoking gun—wearing only my boxers.

12

The sixth precinct police evidence warehouse was little more than a bunker sitting in a corner of the parking lot. It was a flat, one story building made of cinder blocks and those god-awful green glass cubes. The chain-link fence surrounding the warehouse had rusted barbed wire running along the top, but it and the fence were in such bad shape they would probably crumble at the slightest touch, and besides, the gate was open. The steel door of the warehouse was protected by a large but far from unbreakable padlock—nothing that couldn't be snapped with a decent crowbar.

Point being, it would've been easier to bust into the joint than go through all the usual procedural bullshit, but I did it anyway. I knew they had my name and didn't want to get Blout in trouble.

A uniformed flunky unlocked the door, removing the padlock with a lazy yank, then handed me a large ring with one key dangling pathetically from it like a tiny hanged man.

"Lock up when you're finished. The boxes are

alphabetical by last name of victim or perp. If you want to take anything, clear it at the desk," he drawled and walked off, lazy and slack-jawed.

I watched him walk away. He was more dead than any zombie I'd ever encountered. "Thanks a lot, sparkles," I muttered. I was pretty sure he didn't hear.

The big metal door gave me a little trouble at first. I had to push against it with my bum shoulder, but that wasn't enough. So this was the master security system, I thought. How diabolical. The hinges were rusted, so I resorted to kicking. The first two kicks did nothing but send shooting pains up my leg. The third did the trick. The door swung open, sending a cloud of dust billowing into the air.

I coughed and fanned my arms through the soot. The warehouse was dark and smelled of grime, mothballs, and that smoky smell you can only get from old books. I let the door swing shut behind me while I fumbled for a light switch. The low-ceilinged rectangle filled with brownish-yellow light. The place was jam-packed to the roof with rotting cardboard—a total mess.

I doubted anyone had been in here for a long time. I was equally sure the place had been ransacked, with anything even remotely of value stolen. That happened all the time with police evidence. There are cops who use these warehouses as their own personal K-Mart. Luckily, I was looking for books. I was willing to bet that the type of cops who stole police evidence weren't big readers.

The evidence had been stored in alphabetical order as the flunky had said, but only in the most general sense. There were letters of the alphabet painted on the walls, like an underground parking lot. I was amazed at the idiocy of the system. Fortunately, the boxes themselves were labeled, but it was still going to be a major pain in the ass. I took off my jacket, rolled up my sleeves and set about digging into the area around the letter "C."

It took over an hour for me to locate five small boxes labeled as Cain's property. All of the seals were broken, but it didn't look like much had been stolen. I sat down near the door encircled by the boxes, lit a cigarette and took out my flask. After a long satisfying gulp, I dug into the clutter.

I found something curious as soon as I saw the first book title. The rest were much the same. It seemed Cain and I had some shared interests. There were editions I owned myself, titles like *Monsters, Myths and Folklore*, *The Big Book of Spells*, *Modern Witchcraft*, *Ceremonies of Haiti*, and *ESP and Telepathy Today*.

Each of the books was littered with papers marking spots in the pages. On several of the papers, Cain had written notes. It was better than I could have imagined, a friggin' Clues 'R' Us. It seemed odd that the original investigators didn't take notice, but I assumed any further probing might have brought out facts the authorities would rather not know. Besides, who was I to point fingers? I dropped the case as soon as we smashed into the pavement.

The first book I looked over was *ESP and Telepathy Today*, an outdated and sensationalist volume published by a company specializing in books on Bigfoot and UFOs. The paperback was packed with black and white photos and crude drawings that claimed to prove the existence and validity of telepathy, telekinesis and ESP. There were photos of people floating in the air with no visible supports (obviously airbrushed), a man with horned-rimmed glasses and a goatee straining to lift a person with the power of his mind, and that sort of crap.

I actually found myself enjoying flipping through the junky, dog-eared book, just like when I was a kid. True or not, these books had a kind of charm about them that I still found fascinating. Cain seemed to have been especially interested in a section of the book showing a man bending spoons with mind power.

The pages were marked and several photos circled, but nothing seemed overly important, so I closed the book and shoved it into my coat pocket.

Next was *The Big Book of Spells*. Most of it was clean except for a chapter on voodoo that Cain had highlighted and underlined almost completely. The text was very simple, obviously intended for young readers with overwritten, dramatic passages and out-right silly chants purported to evoke the spirits. Cain had circled several of the spells in red.

Early in *Monsters, Myths, and Folklore*, Cain had marked off a two-page spread discussing the Egyptian god Anubis, the jackal-headed god of death. He was often associated with the creation of the art of embalming and was sometimes called the conductor of the dead.

Most of the underlining seemed to revolve around gods of death, reanimation, and resurrection. When I came across the last marked page, the pieces began to fall into place. The passage described the Norse legend of the Yimir. On the edges of the text, Cain had scrawled the words "the first giant," and had underlined "legend says that the clouds are made from the brains of the Yimir." At the bottom of the page he had written down incantations from the voodoo book. Next to some of the spells were page numbers.

I opened the spell book Cain referred to and turned to the indicated pages. The underlined section read "in voodoo, the brain is the seat of animate spirits."

On a Post-it note stuck to the page, Cain linked the passages:

> The brain is the seat of the animate, the soul of all spirits.
> Clouds are made from the brains of the Yimir.
> The Yimir was the first giant.

> The mind is the soul.
> The heart is life.
> Never shall they cross.
> Never will we die.

I had no idea what the hell this all meant, beyond the fact that it was pretty clear he'd been obsessed with witchcraft, voodoo, and resurrection. I began to rethink my earlier deductions about spontaneous phenomenon: there may be a source other than Cain, and he may have even created it, but Cain was dead, definitely dead. I had sat covered in his splattered remains. There was nothing left of him that could even be collected. That final fall we took together had reduced him to a pool of splattered, slimy slop.

I found what I came for. Not a lot of answers, but

a whole lot of clues, and one or two flimsy concepts. I threw the books back into the boxes, keeping all the scraps of paper for myself. Before I left, I rummaged through the boxes one more time.

Good thing too, because I came across something interesting. It was a pair of brown corduroy bell-bottom pants. The fact that somebody actually wore them was amazing enough, but in the back pocket I found Cain's wallet, complete and untouched. The pocket had been snapped shut with those little pocket snaps that they only use on kids slacks. Thank God for small miracles and inept police work. I did wonder how the cops could have possibly missed the wallet, but the reason became immediately clear. There was a skid mark the size of New Jersey that started on the inside of the pants and seeped all the way through to the outside. I dropped that foul shit and prayed my hand hadn't gone near the stain.

Inside the wallet there was, briefly, seventeen bucks. I found Cain's driver's license, but the photo didn't ring any bells. The only time I'd seen him, his head was huge, features stretched and distorted. When I felt along the inside seam of the wallet, I felt a small hard object sewn inside. The seam tore easily and a tiny manila envelope fell out. It hit the cement floor with a muffled clink.

The envelope had the Riggs National Bank logo stamped on it. Inside was a key on a tiny cardboard tag, "G454" written on it. I couldn't help but grin.

13

It was Sunday, so going to the bank was out of the question. Instead, I had another plan. I called my apartment, and after a few rings, Mo'Lock picked up. In the background the TV was blaring so loudly that I could hardly hear the ghoul say hello.

"For Christ sake, Mo'!" I yelled. "Turn down the TV!"

I heard him drop the receiver. Fuckin' ghoul.

The noise cut off abruptly and a second later he was back on the line. "Yes, Cal. What is it?"

"How're you doing?" I asked, "Gun wounds alright?"

"All healed up, but I need a new shirt."

I grinned. "I got a plan. It looks like we've got a little down time on the brainless case, so I thought we could go after the gun happy punks who shot you."

"They're outside again. A little farther down the block, but I can see them."

"Persistent little bastards, aren't they?"

"And not too bright, I'd say. Tell me the plan." He sounded more like a cop than I ever did.

"Simple, get a couple of your friends together. Not a crowd, just one or two—"

The ghoul cut me off. "Since the disappearance of the last two volunteers in the tunnel, I don't think anybody will be up for another mission."

"They're goddamn dead already! What the hell have they got to be scared of?!" I was pissed, and a little embarrassed. I couldn't even get dead guys to help me.

"That's just it, Cal. They have nothing to be afraid of, but they are afraid. We still have gotten no word from the last two and nobody wants to go down there to find out why."

"Pussies. When I get the chance, I'll do it myself. Right now, let's just stop these punks before they get lucky and put a slug in my brain. Are you with me?"

Mo'Lock sounded insulted. "Of course."

"I need you to distract them. Walk by the windows, rustle the shades. I don't care what you do, just keep 'em looking at the apartment. When you see some action, come down and give me a hand."

"I'm on it."

It took me a few minutes to walk from the Dupont Metro station to the street where I lived. I stopped about three blocks back, careful to check everything in my line of vision. Since it was Sunday, the streets were deserted. If bullets started flying, I didn't have to worry about bystanders.

Everything was clear. When I was a block away, I flattened myself against the wall of the building to my left. If Mo'Lock was right, my ascot-wearing would-be assassins were right in the courtyard, near the entrance.

I took out a can of mace and my favorite blackjack. I wanted them alive, if possible. Well, at least one of them. For questioning. If they were working for someone else, I needed to know who it was. If they were operating on their own, I wanted to find out why. After that, I was just going to beat the living crap out of them for fun.

I peered, one-eyed, around the corner. They were there, all three of them, staring up at the window of my place. I started moving around the corner, edging slowly so as not to catch their attention. I made the mistake of following their gaze and almost laughed out loud.

Mo'Lock was thrashing wildly from window to window. It looked like he was doing a super-charged dance of the veils. I forced myself to look away and focus on the perps.

They wore the same clothes as the day before, with

one exception—the female had a bandage around her head. I could see a spot of blood where one of my shots must have grazed her.

I crept up until I was right behind her, but she turned quickly. The look on her face when she saw me was reward enough, but I popped her anyway. One swipe with the blackjack and she hit the ground like a wet teabag. Her two buddies spun around and I was in trouble instantly. Caught with no room to move and no time to reach for my piece, I did what seemed to be the only thing that made any sense.

I screamed for the ghoul to back me up.

"Mo'Lock!"

Yelling stalled the two boys for half a second. I was about to mace them to hold them at bay while I awaited tall-dead-and-ugly, but the sight of their faces made me hesitate. They were beyond strange, like plastic or wax, but very, very pretty. Like models straight out of a glossy advertisement, every feature was carved perfection. I began to realize who these oddly beautiful teens might be.

One of the lovelies broke my reverie by pulling a small silver pistol. The look on his face was anything but attractive as he lowered it and fired. I dodged but the bullet hit the exact spot of the first bullet wound, an unbelievable bull's-eye. To describe the pain would be impossible. Suffice to say, I screamed.

The kid never got off a second shot. Mo'Lock had arrived via the window. He was on the armed kid like stink on shit, a flailing angry marionette, hitting the shooter while kicking the other male, the only blonde of the three, in the lower back. Blondie hit the ground, and I followed up with a smack from the blackjack, hitting him square in the mouth. His teeth blew apart like china tea cups, raining on the street with a hundred gentle tinkles. It was incredible.

Mo'Lock was out of control. He had the kid over his head. I wanted to say something, but it was too late. The ghoul threw pretty boy through the Mustang's windshield and the brief skirmish came to a sudden and resounding halt. All we needed to do was get the three of them up to my place for a little chitchat. I grabbed the girl and toothless and left Mo'Lock to deal with the one wedged in the windshield.

The trio slept for awhile, giving us time to tie them to chairs after patching them up. Mo'Lock played nurse, applying cold packs and bandages to their bruises. As they began to stir, I removed their ascots and wristbands. What I saw underneath, just below the neckline of their shirts, cleared up a mystery I had been trying to resolve for years and confirmed the hunch I got when I first saw their faces.

Wrapping all the way around each of their wrists and throats were very faint but visible stitch scars—scars from where the body parts had been grafted together by Dr. Polynice at the request of Francis Lazar, founder of ManChildLove. Tied to chairs in my apartment were the mail-order Voodoo Love Teens, kids that those two creeps had created. I'd broken the case wide open and sent Lazar, Polynice, and all those involved to prison, including anyone who had ordered a love slave, but not a trace of the teens had ever been found.

Until today.

I stared at their chiseled features. If you looked very closely you could see faint signs of plastic surgery. It was very important to Lazar and the good doctor that the love dolls could never be traced to the original victims. Their entire bodies, including their heads and facial features, were a jumbled mishmash of dissected, murdered young men and women, complete with burned off fingerprints and brittle teeth.

The teeth were a nice touch—you've gotta admire attention to detail. Fake teeth meant no dental records. They must've used porcelain for that perfect white color. Evidently, being smacked in the mouth with a blackjack wasn't in the plans.

Windshield was the first to come around. He shook his head, blinked, and blew his dark hair away from his eyes that were a deep, unnatural navy blue. They locked on me immediately. The look was pure hatred.

"You got a name?" I asked, indifferent to the boy's glare. I was standing with one foot up on a chair, interrogation style.

"Randy."

I was surprised. The kid gave up his name easily. I suspect that was part of the conditioning they went through before they were sold off. Nobody likes a difficult love doll.

The whole thing made me sick to my stomach, and it wasn't just me. Mo'Lock seemed uneasy around the kids. He muttered under his breath about tormented souls before retiring to his corner and staring out the window. I didn't have that luxury. If I didn't do something now, these damn kids would never stop coming after me.

I got on with it. "You know who I am?"

Randy nodded, with his glaring blue eyes fixed on my face. "Cal McDonald," he said. "You took my father away... took away all our parents. Took away Lazar and everybody!"

I shook my head and paced a small circle. This was going to be tough. "What your 'parents' did was wrong, not to mention illegal and highly immoral. Lazar was a bad person who had to be stopped."

"He never hurt anyone! He took care of us when nobody else would, and he found us homes!"

The other two had begun to stir. The female was muttering and her head swayed side to side.

This was going to be difficult. Very, very difficult. The kids probably had no idea what they were or where they came from. I had to be careful. Mo'Lock turned to me and shrugged his wide bony shoulders, offering me no help. I couldn't determine whether the ghoul couldn't or wouldn't. He seemed edgy about the whole thing, edgy and distant.

I paced a little, then went back to Randy and stood in front of him holding my hand on my chin.

"Can you tell me how old you are, Randy?"

The kid dropped the glare and thought about the question.

"I think… yes, I'm sure. I'm five years old." His face lit up with pride.

I shook my head. "Don't you think you're a little big for a five-year-old."

Randy looked at me, incredulous to my query. "No," he said, "all of my brothers and sisters are five."

By now the other two were conscious and listening. Neither had the rage in their eyes that Randy had. Just the opposite, actually. They seemed scared of me. I counted myself lucky for that. It meant if I could get through to Randy, the others would most likely follow. I scrambled for questions.

"Can you tell me how you were born?"

The boy looked at me like I was the dumbest thing he'd ever laid eyes on. All three smiled, enjoying their little in-joke.

"In the lab," Randy said sarcastically, "Where else?"

Blondie and the girl suppressed laughter.

I nodded. Lazar and Polynice had done a real job on these kids. They had no concept of the real world, just the twisted reality created for them. In desperation, I looked at Mo'Lock again—I was out of ideas. "What do you think, Mo'?"

"They are very scary, Cal. Do you realize between the three of them, they share the fragments of over one hundred tormented souls."

"Fucking-A. What we can do? How can we make them see what's really happening? They don't even know what they are!" I could hear the desperation in my own voice.

Mo'Lock turned and stared at the three teens who

were whispering to each other, seemingly unaffected by the fact they were tied up.

"They're not stupid, Cal. Show them the file, the articles, the whole mess. Let them see for themselves."

He was right.

I told Mo'Lock to untie Randy's arms so he could flip freely through the files, but to make sure his legs were secure. I didn't want the little punk running off on us. Meanwhile, I ransacked the file cabinets for everything I had on the Lazar case.

While I was rooting around, I glanced over and saw Randy staring fascinated at Mo'Lock. Mo'Lock met the kid's eyes and did something that was all too rare for a ghoul, and truly gave me pause. He smiled. Slight, but distinct. His dead lips parted, curving slowly upwards. His eyes, usually stone cold, opened wider and brightened.

I was a minority in the room. The others were cousins in a very large and odd clan—the family of the living dead.

When I'd gathered all the Lazar/Polynice files, I dropped them in Randy's lap. He no longer glared at me. In fact all three seemed much less hostile. They were like putty, instantly impressionable, easily swayed. Nonetheless, I wasn't about to untie anybody until after they'd read the files. I had no idea what the reaction would be, but it was reasonable to assume a violent one.

All eyes were on Randy. He began reading the police report, slowly scanning the pages. At first he seemed calm seeing the photos of the men who had created and sold him for a profit. He almost had a look of love in his eyes. But as he began to soak everything in, his features hardened. Word after word, paragraph after paragraph, page after page had a visible affect on him. He began to shake as pages turned. Finally the tremors were so bad he could no longer hold onto a file. I stood by uncomfortably. Mo'Lock rocked foot to foot behind me. There was nothing we could do but wait for the reaction, the inevitable explosion.

When it came it was fast and loud. Randy's eyes began to well. He looked up at me first, then shot quick glances at Mo'Lock and I, eyes overflowing with tears. It was as if his soul were bleeding out his tear-ducts.

"Who am I?" he asked.

For that, I had no answer... but Mo'Lock did.

Mo'Lock stepped past me, stopping close to the weeping boy. The other two had started crying as well, but I doubt they knew why. Fuckin' puppets.

Mo'Lock got down on one knee and addressed his distant cousin.

"You are many people and many souls. You are bound by the bodies that have been assembled for you. There is no changing this. You must accept what you are... as I have."

Randy stuttered and stammered before finally collecting himself enough to speak. "You... you're like us?"

The ghoul nodded. "In a sense. I too used to be mortal, but then I died. Though my soul departed, I remained. Now I am undead. What happened to all of you was brought on by the magic of a conjurer, and now you too are undead. Trust me when I tell you... being dead is not at all a bad thing to be."

He spoke in such a confident manner, oddly poetic in a scary sort of way. His voice was soothing, gently guiding the zombie youth to the realization that although they were created from evil they did not have to follow its twisted course. That was the great lie to which too many monsters, past and present, had fallen prey.

They were quickly convinced, maybe because they were made that way, maybe because we offered them an alternative future. I wasn't about to question it, though. I'd expected much worse.

I was still uneasy, but Mo'Lock assured me they were okay now, so I reluctantly loosened their bindings. Sure enough, they'd been defanged.

Randy introduced the others. Blondie was Scott, and the girl was Miriam. I shook each of their hands as they apologized for trying to kill me.

"Don't sweat it." I said. This whole situation was fucking surreal. I grabbed the bottle from my desk and took several large mouthfuls until it was empty. I hadn't eaten, so I felt instantly buzzed.

Twenty minutes passed without anyone saying a word. Mo'Lock and I realized the poor kids had spent so long tracking me down that they had no other experience whatsoever. The three of them sat there, free of the ropes, but with no reason to stand and nowhere to go.

"What do we do now?" Randy said.

Maybe it was only a drunken brainstorm, but I had an idea. I weaved out of the room and came back a minute later with the Yellow Pages. I tore a page out and handed it to Randy. He was confused at first, but a smile soon grew across his lips.

"What do you think?" I asked.

He showed Scott and Miriam the page. They all smiled.

Miriam looked at me. "That would be fun. Do you think we can?"

"I think you'd be perfect."

The beautiful voodoo teens were absolutely giddy. Mo'Lock was confused.

"Mo'Lock, how much cash do you have?"

He shrugged. "Couple hundred."

"Can you get these guys set up someplace? One of your ghoul flophouses or something?"

Everybody was happy. Mo'Lock agreed to leave with the trio and find them a place to crash, but after ushering the group out the door he popped his head back inside as I was taking a seat at the desk.

"What was on that page, Cal?" he asked peering around the door.

"Modeling agencies. I figured once they healed, they'd clean up pretty good as models," I said. "Always attractive. Never age."

He mulled it over for a minute, then nodded. "Good going, Cal. Good for you," he said and was gone.

I admit that I felt pretty damn good after that. For once I didn't have to kill something to solve a problem. It's not often in my line of work that there's a happy ending. I celebrated with a Vicodin, a pop of crank, and a big sloppy gyro I had delivered, along with a huge, heart-stopping pile of cheese fries.

14

The good feelings lasted for as long as it took the phone to ring—four blissful days. Then on Thursday, Blout called and broke the spell.

"Big trouble!" he yelled. I'd never heard him so agitated.

"Calm the fuck down! What's up?"

"Tourists are dropping like goddamn flies down on the Mall. We've got ten down in Natural History and the 911 switchboards are lighting up! I'm heading down there."

Christ, I thought, it was just like Whitney Green all those years ago. "Here we go again. I guess whatever is behind this is up to steam. Listen, do you have any painkillers or some liquor there with you?"

"Yeah, sure… why?!"

"Do me a favor, before you go down there, have a drink or a pill or sniff some glue. I don't care, just do something that clouds your mind. It won't take you if your brain is damaged."

"Please, Cal, shut the fuck up. I called for help."

He wasn't buying it. "Think of the dope as a Kevlar vest for your brain."

Blout paused. For once he didn't argue. "Whatever."

I told him I had an errand to run, that it was

important to the case and that I'd be down as soon as I could.

Speed and a pot of black coffee got me to work making some changes on Edgar Cain's driver's license. I altered the expiration date and popped in my photo. Kid stuff really, and when the job was done it looked damn convincing. There'd be no trouble at the bank.

As I was about to leave, Mo'Lock came through the door.

"Good," I said, "I'm glad you're here. We got bad news."

"I know. My brothers and sisters are fleeing the city. There's a major disturbance. Any leads?"

"Leads I got. Answers, not a one" I rubbed my face. "Everything points to Edgar Cain, but—"

"He's dead," Mo' said and then, "He is dead, right?"

I looked up. "That's the one thing I am sure of. There was nothing left of him, not enough to even collect for evidence. The fire department had to wash the gunk off the streets with their hoses…"

I stopped. If my head could have turned into a jackass head, it would have. Mo'Lock finished my thought.

"Into the sewers."

I rubbed my eyes. "Why do they always go in the sewers."

15

I had what I thought was a decent plan, but first, I had to get to the bank. I had a pretty good hunch what was in that safe deposit box, and we'd need it to survive what was to come. After that, there was no avoiding it. The ghoul and I had to go down into the sewers.

Mo'Lock and I agreed to meet at the drainage pipe a few hours later. After he left, I checked to make sure I was properly armed. Fuck yeah, I must have weighed an extra ten pounds with all my extra baggage. I made sure I had the safe deposit key and the talisman Mo' had found.

As an extra precaution, I slipped a small leather case that I kept for years into my sock.

Everything was in place. I was as ready as I'd ever be. But before I could get out the office door, I had company.

Dan Stockton, that huge prick of a cop, standing there blocking my exit, with two other uniforms behind him.

I motioned to push past. Stockton blocked my way.

"I don't have time for this shit, Stockton. Get out of my way. We can fight later." I made another move, he countered. This time he held up a folded document.

"This ain't personal," Stockton said, waving the papers in my face. "This is straight up official. I've got a warrant for your arrest."

I stepped back. All three pressed forward. I could see that the two back-ups were taking out their batons. One had handcuffs ready for me.

"Arrest? What the hell for?!"

Stockton smirked. "You had a court date yesterday with some guy you pummeled on Halloween, and you were a no-show. That, my asshole friend, is against the law."

"Moving a little fast, aren't they?" I said.

Stockton's smirk widened to an outright obnoxious grin. "That's the personal part. I did the paperwork myself."

"Gee, thanks."

The scene froze while everybody waited for something to happen. I made it happen by bolting for the door. I broke the blue-boy wall, catching them off-guard. Stockton made a stupid choking sound as I brushed past, as though he couldn't believe he'd lost control of the situation. Idiot.

I was at the door, almost to the hallway. Once there, I could really haul ass. "I told you I don't have time for this sh—" That was that.

For the second goddamn time in under a month, I was knocked cold.

16

I woke in a small room that reeked of body odor and cigarettes, handcuffed to a loop in the wall. I was kneeling, facing the loop, with my back to the rest of the cramped room. The only way in or out—a heavy, industrial-strength door—was behind me. The brick walls were spotted with traces of blood that had been lazily wiped off and covered by a thin coat of off-white.

Standard interrogation procedure. They wanted you to see the blood so you'd start shitting yourself before they even hit you. I'd been through it before, but had a bad feeling about this. Something felt very wrong.

My wrists were bleeding from the cuffs that supported most of my weight and the back of my head stung from where Stockton had planted his nightstick. It made me think of those kids and how I'd walloped them with my blackjack. I was about to feel bad about it when the door behind me opened. I didn't twist around to see who it was. I already knew.

"Thought you'd never wake up," Stockton said behind me.

"Gotta get my beauty sleep."

I heard him shut the door, then a hard *clack* as the lock slipped onto place. "You're gonna go out smart-assin', huh?"

Go out? What the hell was he talking about? I mean, we didn't like each other, but this was out of left field. Years of unfriendly snips, the occasional fisticuffs was one thing. This was beyond bitter dislike. This was nuts. I began to feel scared for the first time in a long while.

"You know, Stocky," I said, "this kind of thing is frowned upon these days. I could sue." I was half telling the truth, half fishing. I heard my voice shake.

He grabbed me by the hair and jerked my face around to his. He was red-faced and spitting. "Not if you're dead, funny man!"

"Have you considered an anger management course?"

That was the last thing I remember saying. The next twenty minutes were a blur of kicks and punches. Stockton was good at it. He knew all the places to hit and just how hard to strike for maximum pain. I just went limp and tried not to make a sound. I figured even a raging psycho like him would get sick of beating on a wet sack of mud after a while.

But he just went on and on until my face was puffed like a bloody bunt-cake and my body was tender to the touch. What amazed me even as I was being beat was his skill at keeping me conscious. He wanted me awake, and awake I stayed. Finally he tired of hitting me and pulled a blade from his back pocket.

I spat a wad of thick blood. "Come on, Stockton. You made your point."

He ignored me. "You ever hear of ham-stringing? It's supposed to hurt a lot."

I shivered. Nobody walks after having the backs of their knees sliced. If he truly meant to hamstring me, I was through.

Luckily, I have a merciful angel that watches over me. That angel happens to be a big cop named Jefferson Blout.

My eyes were nearly swollen shut, but I heard him come crashing into that room like a diesel. I had the pleasure of hearing Stockton give a little baby yelp right before Blout shattered his jaw with a roundhouse punch that would have made a Viking weep. It was beautiful.

When it was all said and done, I was banged up pretty good, but I could still walk. Blout talked me into going to the hospital where I got a couple dozen stitches and a jumbo Band-Aid or two. I made sure to whine until the doctor ordered some painkillers, so in the end I came out okay. Shit, I'd gone through a lot worse to get drugs before.

Blout was waiting for me outside.

"So how the hell did you know Stockton had me dragged in?" I asked. His appearance had been nothing short of miraculous.

"A rook tipped me off. He wasn't too keen on losing his badge so Stockton could waste some lousy gumshoe."

"Thanks."

"His words, not mine." But he enjoyed telling me. I could see it in his face.

"So what's the word on the deaths at the Mall?"

"Not as bad as I thought. Eight, maybe nine."

"Skulls?"

"Clean."

I nodded. "It's revving up for the big strike."

Blout rammed one of his cigars into his mouth and lit it. "What are you talking about now?"

"What we're dealing with here played it safe for a few years. It plucked the brains out of people who never went through full autopsies, like chronic cases and the elderly. Then it moved on to the homeless."

I paused and lit a cigarette of my own.

"Now it's getting up some speed and hitting tourists, and soon it's going to bust loose and then... the whole city's fair game."

I thought Blout was going to bust my chops, but instead he shook his head. "Christ. What are we dealing with here? Do you have any ideas at all?"

"It's Cain," I said.

"The dead man?"

"The dead man."

"You want to tell me how?"

"Would it matter?"

Blout thought about getting pissed, but he didn't have the strength. He just nodded a sad little nod and bit his lip.

As we got to Blout's ugly car, he gave me back all the stuff the cops confiscated—gun, blackjack, fake ID and safe deposit key. Asshole held back two items, though, wanting answers before he'd hand them over. I was in no shape to fight, so I'd play his little game.

He opened one of his big hands, revealing the leather case I'd stashed in my sock. It was my old friends: syringe, spoon, and smack. I couldn't believe Blout had retrieved it for me. In the other hand he clutched the talisman Mo'Lock had ripped off the tunnel zombie.

"Where do I start?"

"How about the works?" Blout said. "Don't tell me you're doing shit again."

I shook my head and spoke, praying my voice didn't slur from the painkillers. "Remember what I told you? That last time I dealt with Cain? It didn't absorb my brain because it disliked the pollution. I just have it on me as a precaution. I swear." My hand was raised like a Boy Scout, and I tried to force a brown-nose smile across my beaten, puffy face.

He seemed satisfied enough and tossed me the case. "Thought you'd say that. Only as a last resort, you got it?" he said. Then he held up the talisman. "And this?"

"Mo'Lock found it in the tunnels beneath Whitney Green." I looked down at the ground.

"Tunnels beneath Whitney Green? Hmmm, I don't recall you mentioning anything about tunnels," he spoke in mock tones of mystery. Then he screamed, *"YOU FUCK!"* and rammed his palm right into my wounded shoulder.

I yelled out.

"What else aren't you telling me? Goddammit, Cal! Stop keeping me in the dark! What good am I if I only know half the story?"

I looked up, rubbing my shoulder. "Sorry. I'm not

used to letting cops in on this kind of stuff. I think you'll recall what happened the few times I did. I got laughed right off the case."

Blout took a couple of angry puffs off his log of a cigar. "Well that was them, this is me. Cough it up."

He was right. Where would I be if he hadn't informed me of the mysterious deaths when he did? I told him everything I knew, about Mo'Lock and the crusty tunnel zombies who had attacked us, and about the missing ghouls. I filled him in on Cain and what I found in the evidence room. When I was finished he tossed me the talisman.

"What about this, then? How does that fit it?"

I looked at the charm. "Considering the thing wearing it turned into a pool of blood when it was removed, I'd say it's a resurrection talisman. Black magic, voodoo maybe. I can't say for sure."

"Did you notice something floating in the liquid?"

"Yeah, but I couldn't make it out. Probably a piece of bone." I stuffed the charm into my pocket considering the issue closed and moot.

"It's an Egyptian symbol," Blout said plainly.

"Huh? How'd you know?" I was stunned.

"My wife collects all kinds of that ugly crap. The house was full of it. The living room looked like friggin' King Tut's tomb. That shit was gone the moment she left."

I had to laugh. "Any idea what it means?"

"The perp shops at the same place as Jessica?"

"Now who's the smart ass? So what we're left with here is a mix of black magic, monsters and myth, voodoo of several varieties, and now Egyptian symbols. That's the oddest, because the Egyptians weren't into reviving dead. All their ceremonies revolved around surviving the afterlife. Even this talisman's a little bit this, a little bit that—a goddamn potpourri of evil." I scratched my aching head. "Oh yeah, and we have a giant brain-sucking head that should be dead but somehow isn't."

I needed to get moving to clear my head. With all the time wasted getting the crap beat out of me, I'd have to hustle to meet the ghoul at the drainage pipe. I told Blout to drop me off at Riggs while he went on to meet Mo'Lock and tell him to wait until I arrived. Blout wasn't thrilled with the plan.

"No way," he said. "I'm not going near that freak without you. I'll check the box. You take the car to the pipe."

I tried chiding him. "Are you scared?"

He pulled the wheel extra hard on a left turn, slamming my head against the window frame. "I wouldn't call it scared, punching bag. More like creeped out."

"Splitting hairs." I gingerly touched the swell of bruises on the side of my face. "Besides, you might not like what you find in the box." I tried to sound ominous, but I came off more like Bob Barker. My mouth was too swollen.

Blout gave out a quick breathy laugh. "I'll take my chances. And to be on the safe side, I won't look inside until I meet you back at the drainage pipe."

"They are not going to let you walk out of the bank with the whole safe deposit box." I started laughing, knowing full well what was coming next.

He turned to me. A big toothy grin was spread across his face. "Wanna bet?"

17

Blout screeched up to the curb in front of the bank. He got out with the car running, keys dangling in the ignition. I scooted across the seat and pulled the door shut. Instead of charging into the bank as I'd hoped, Blout stood there shuffling his feet. It didn't take a brain surgeon to see he was nervous with me behind the wheel of his butt-ugly car.

"Are you okay? For driving, I mean. What did they give you back at the hospital?"

I let my head bob out of control. "I'm phhhhine! Don't worry about a phhhhing!" I fell against the wheel, sounding the horn for a good thirty seconds. Fun, but we were losing time. "Seriously. We've got work to do. I'm fine and I'm late."

I floored it, leaving Blout breathing exhaust. When I glanced back, he was flipping me off, both hands raised above the smoke. I laughed, but the seriousness of the situation began to sink in. I was through joking for the moment.

I glanced down at the dashboard and saw one of those cheap plastic stick-on digital clocks just above the ashtray. If the clock was right, I was over half an hour late. Mo'Lock would wait, that much I could rely on. He had the patience of a dead man.

I drove carefully, taking the back streets past Dupont Circle straight up Connecticut Avenue until I was near Embassy Row. Once I was clear of the major urban areas I pulled over and parked in front of a liquor store. Not only was I shaky, but a head-ache had begun creeping up on me, moving around like a probing flashlight beam. In the liquor store, I purchased two pints of rotgut—one for me and one for Blout.

In the car I popped a couple of pills from the hospital and washed it down with the booze. It occurred to me it might not be safe to mix the two, but I figured the results would become apparent soon enough.

It took about ten minutes to arrive at the old reservoir off Wisconsin Avenue. From the street it looked like a small lake, but when you got close you could see a cement bottom and surrounding fence. Problem was, it took eight minutes for the mystery of mixing drugs and alcohol to be solved. It wasn't good. I was dizzy, my head was reeling and I couldn't feel my teeth.

I steered the car around the chain-link fence and cruised along the elevated access road, raising roostertails worthy of a *Dukes of Hazard* episode. The drainage pipe was far from the main road and more or less hidden from public view. In my drugged haze, I'd let the car drift to where the shoulder dropped away from the road surface. I took a sharp right to bring the car back parallel with the pipe while jamming on the brakes, but it was too little too late.

The big car skidded over the edge sideways, jumped and began to turn over. It rolled with me trapped inside being flipped and flopped around like socks in the dryer. With a sickening crunch all motion ceased as I arrived at the drainage pipe. The car came to a halt on its roof a few yards short of the pipe's entrance. Totaled, crushed like an accordion. Blout was going to kill me!

I was pinned, but could hear voices outside. It was Mo'Lock for sure and, from the sound of it, he'd found some backup. And there I was, the big leader, trapped in a borrowed car that I had driven into a ditch. What an entrance.

I was relieved to see that neither of the bottles had gotten smashed in the crash. The talisman, however, hadn't been so lucky. My pants had a dark sticky wet spot seeping through the pocket.

I kicked at one of the back doors while Mo'Lock

pulled from the outside. Finally I was able to crawl free into the hazy daylight.

Mo'Lock's big pale face was right there. "Is this Mr. Blout's car?"

"It was."

"He's going to kill you."

I ignored the comment as I dusted myself off, noticing the volunteer army Mo'Lock had assembled; the Frankenteens Scott and Miriam and a large ghoul I'd never met. The unknown ghoul was huge, with wide shoulders, big hands and a head that looked like a cement block with slits for eyes and a dark flat-top.

Mo'Lock did the introductions. "Cal, this is Hank Gundy. He's offered his services. I'm afraid all my brothers and sisters refused."

I shook the behemoth's hand. "You're not a ghoul?"

Gundy shook his head. "Not ghoul," he said. "Hank a creep."

I shot Mo'Lock a quizzical look.

He waved me off. "I'll explain later."

I swear, there are more varieties of monster than there are insects. Even with all my years of dealing with the shit I still don't know them all.

I turned my attention to the teens. "Thanks for coming," I said. "Where's... um, Windshield?"

"Randy," they both said.

Miriam smiled. "He got a gig!"

Not really wanting to hear more, I ushered everyone to the tunnel mouth. Mo'Lock had outlined what he knew of the plan—the layout of the tunnels and the static he'd encountered—and I filled them in on the rest. The teens seemed to understand everything, but Gundy kept looking around distracted. It didn't matter. I suspected that if and when there was trouble he'd know what to do.

"I don't know what we're going to find down there. All I do know is that it involves many, many forms of witchcraft and dark arts, so be ready for anything. Most important of all: if anybody's head starts to hurt, drop back."

Mo'Lock edged up close as I finished my instructions. "Do you see them?"

I whispered back out of the corner of my mouth, "Yup, been there for the last ten minutes."

Just inside the tunnel, where light stopped and darkness began, stood a wall of empty-eyed zombies.

"We've got some company." I pointed them out to the rest of our crew.

Scott stepped forward. "Those are the things that attacked you?"

Mo'Lock and I both nodded.

I took out my gun, an unreturned police issue

.9mm, and aimed into the crowd at head level. Although I was wasted, my aim was steady as I squeezed off two quick bursts. One of the zombies' heads snapped back violently, and his body quickly fell to the ground like a rag doll. The others went wild, moaning and beating on each other. They wouldn't cross into the light, but wouldn't retreat either. Then the one I shot stood back up with a big chunk of skull missing, only seconds after the gunfire's echo had faded.

I turned to Mo'Lock and Gundy. "This looks like your kinda job."

Mo'Lock led Gundy inside and pointed, making sure the big guy was looking. "See those necklaces they're wearing?"

"Around stinky man's necks?"

"Yes?"

Gundy nodded.

"You and I are going to run in there and grab as many as we can. It kills them. Got that?"

Gundy sharpened at the prospect of violence. "Got it. Hank take necklace. Stinky man die."

"Let's go," said the ghoul.

They charged into the tunnel, leaving me and the Frankenteens behind to watch and pray. It took only seconds for them to hit the zombie wall. From my vantage point, it looked like a riot had erupted: I couldn't even make out the shapes of Mo'Lock and Gundy as the crowd consumed them. Amidst the furor, though, I heard sounds that hinted at some level of success. There was a distinct slopping and sloshing sound of thick liquid being spilled. Those things were going down in gobs of blood.

Problem was, there seemed to be too damn many of them. I got panicky and pulled my gun out again, edging into the tunnel along the wall. I began shooting into the crowd, thinking it served as a distraction if nothing else.

From inside the tunnel, we heard Mo'Lock shout, "We could use some help in here!"

I was glad to oblige, but Miriam and Scott didn't share my eagerness. They were scared stiff. I ran into the tunnel without them, itching for some payback. I planned to blast first, then tear away their talismans before they could recover. I started shooting as I ran, but my heel hit a thick dark puddle and sent me sliding top speed into the thick of the fray. Through it all, I'd never stopped firing.

I clamored to my feet, but they were on me instantly. I remembered their dry, crusty touch from the stairwell. That time they'd blindsided me. This would be different.

I let them kick and punch at me. I didn't care. All I wanted was a handful of leather, a sliver of glass in my palm. When I had it, I yanked. Time after time, I'd hear a satisfying yelp followed by the sound of hot stew hitting the floor, then I'd grab for more. It was like flushing away the enemy, one of the most satisfying fights I ever had.

I hardly noticed when it was over, with the last dozen or so zombies retreating into the inner depths of the tunnels. Suddenly there was pin drop silence. I looked around. Mo'Lock was nearby with two fistfuls of necklaces, Gundy was behind us. In one hand he had necklaces, but the other held a leg. I looked down and saw we were up to our ankles in liquified zombie blood. It was fucking disgusting.

We left the tunnel to gather ourselves as Mo'Lock giddily enthused about all the souls that now had a chance to be free.

It took a moment before we noticed Gundy wasn't following. When we turned, the big guy hadn't moved an inch, hovering on the razor's edge of shadow and light.

"Gundy? You okay?" I yelled.

I could see his big face even at a distance. His expression was like a baby about to cry. He dropped the leg and placed a big hand to his head.

"Head hurts," He said.

And that was that. Big Hank Gundy dropped dead where he stood. I didn't need to see his cracked-open skull to know the brains were gone, completely empty save for the thick curl of steam that slowly snaked from the empty skull cavity.

"Fuck," I said.

We'd wait for Blout before we made our next move.

18

I was pissed about Gundy's death, if that's what you can call it—I never did find out exactly what a creep was. I hadn't even known the guy for ten minutes and now he was a stiff.

I told the Frankenteens to get the hell home. I wasn't going to risk the kids, not after all they'd been through. Luckily, it took little convincing. They wanted to leave.

Like that, my pathetic army was cut in half. It was just me and Mo'Lock again. No one spoke, so I took the time to smoke and have few drinks. I fished the leather case out of my sock, unzipped it and stared at the contents.

"What's that?" Mo'Lock asked. He shambled through the dirt and sat next to me.

I zipped the case and tucked it back in my sock. "Backup plan."

Before he could ask any more questions, we heard a car door slam a short distance away. Blout was walking briskly up the dirt road with the safe deposit box tucked under his arm as the cab returned to the city.

He spotted his car lying upside down at the bottom of the ditch and slowed, shoulders slumping noticeably at the sight. I was afraid he'd drop the box but he clutched it tightly. I watched and waited, half expecting an attack.

"Nice parking space, asshole."

I apologized profusely, but Blout wanted none of it. He was focused on the task at hand, saving all his anger for a fresh new ulcer. For whatever reason, he'd been surprising me lately. Maybe he could sense some bad shit coming. I know I felt it.

The box under his arm was large, much bigger than the proverbial breadbox. True to his word, Blout hadn't opened it. He placed it down in the dust outside the tunnel, glanced inside at the aftermath of the fight and sat down on the ground with a grunt.

"Christ, my head is pounding," He said.

My head was hurting too, but I was still under the protection of a painkiller and alcohol cocktail. I handed Blout the pint I'd picked up for him. He took it and drank the thing down like sugar water. That should do the trick, I thought. If it didn't, I'd get him out of there, like it or not. Even if I had to knock him out, I was not going to have a repeat of Gundy. Not with Blout anyway.

Mo'Lock was shifting on his feet with an expression that I'd never seen before—discomfort. I doubted very seriously that the ghoul was constipated. It had to be his head.

I went to his side. "What's up, Mo'? How're you feeling?"

He looked at me. "I'm not sure… it's been so long, but I think I have a headache."

I took the other pint out of my coat pocket. I'd drank some, but most of it was still there. I forced the bottle into his big white hands.

"Take it. Drink," I demanded.

The ghoul looked at the bottle and grimaced. He shook his head.

"It can't hurt you," I said. "Better safe than sorry."

The ghoul was a sucker for clichés. He looked at the bottle like a boxer

staring down his opponent. I guess I understood. It had been over a century since he had a drink and his first one was about to be some cheap rotgut.

I glanced over at Blout and saw his face was lazy and calm. His eyes were blood-shot and hooded. He had the look of a man with a poisoned brain—our best defense.

"AAAAAHHHHGGGHHHH!!"

Blout and I jumped, simultaneously pulling out our weapons, but it was just Mo'Lock. He'd swigged the entire bottle in one huge gulp and now stood swaying with wide, crazy eyes. I lowered my gun first and with my free hand slowly guided Blout's down to his side. He wasn't so sure there was no reason to shoot.

Blout and I stood by as the ghoul went through a series of shudders and twitches, until gradually the liquor slipped through his ancient veins and his dark-circled eyes reddened.

I waited a few minutes, then took the bottle from him. "How does it feel?"

I asked.

"I feel stupid."

"Perfect."

I rubbed my head and looked from one bleary partner to the other. Blout was trying to find the end of a cigar and having a hard time of it. He'd chugged his entire bottle. Mo'Lock was pressing a finger into his forehead and sticking his tongue out in response to each touch. I sighed. Here we were, the city's heroes. We were doomed.

There was no use wasting any more time. I picked up the safe deposit box and headed into the mouth of the drainage pipe. When I turned, no one else had moved. They were just staring at me blankly.

"Well," I said, "Time to move, you buckin' fastards!"

With that they both shook themselves out of their individual hazes and followed me into the tunnel. Not one of us could walk a straight line.

19

We walked deep into the tunnel, sloshing through the remains of the zombie guards, until the entrance was a pea-sized dot of light behind us. I lit a cigarette and waited for our eyes to adjust to the pitch dark. When Blout's outline became clearer I could see he was agitated and nervous.

"When are you going to open that thing?" he asked, pointing at the box.

I shrugged. "We could do it now if you want. I've got a pretty good idea what's inside."

I felt the key slap against the side of my face and I managed to catch it before it hit the dirt. When I leaned down to feel for the keyhole, I was too ripped and had little luck. My hand clanked the key clumsily against the metal, finding everything except its target.

"You want some light?" Blout switched on his penlight as he knelt down beside me.

"Thanks."

I found the lock and gave it a twist. The box opened with one quick flip, releasing a billowing mushroom of putrescence into the air.

Blout reeled away. "Aw, Jesus!"

I covered my mouth and nose, but the odor was so strong it stung my eyes and forced me to back away from the box. After a second or two the mist cleared and the stench was reduced enough to make it bearable. We knelt and stared down at the throbbing contents of Edgar Cain's safe deposit box. At first glance, it reminded me of those old fifties ads for meat: the colors were too bright and the sheen looked greasy and unreal. But it was real, and it was alive.

A beating human heart.

The disembodied heart rose and fell as if it were still part of a person, still attached to arteries pulsing with blood. Surrounding the heart was a garnish of objects that ranged from feathers to bones. Symbols from a variety of regions and religions were scrawled on paper and wood. It was the same pattern as everything else.

I looked up to Blout. He couldn't take his eyes off the beating heart. Then he caught my stare.

"Is this what you expected?" he stammered.

"I had a hunch it would be something of this sort."

Blout looked back at the heart. "If this is Cain's heart, why don't we just destroy it?"

It was a good question, but not a safe option. Sometimes hearts are not only used to keep something alive, but also to imprison something or keep it in check. We couldn't be sure which kind this was.

"Cain may have put this heart here to protect himself from what was happening," I concluded.

"He didn't do a very good job," Blout said.

Mo'Lock raised a finger. "It could also work to our benefit to have the heart alive, if it is the heart of the killer. It would give us leverage. A hostage, if you will."

So it was agreed—the heart would keep beating for now. I locked up the box and we all headed deeper into the tunnel.

We walked on, deeper and deeper, and I cursed myself for not buying more liquor. I had no idea how long the effects of the alcohol would protect us, and finding out might mean dying. I thought about the leather case in my sock, but shoved the thought away. That was the last resort. Anyway, I still had seven painkillers. If the pain got bad enough I'd convince Blout or the ghoul to take one, like it or not.

I laughed darkly to myself, thinking that only I could stumble onto a case where excessive drug and alcohol use was the best way to stay alive. But here I was with a straight-arrow cop and a hundred-year-old ghoul, drunk in the sewers beneath the nation's capital.

Finally, after what seemed like hours, we came to the intersection Mo'Lock had described last week. I saw the crudely cut hole, definitely not the work of a pro. The edges were rough and jagged and we had to be careful stepping through.

Like the hole itself, the tunnel on the other side was rough hewn. The walls were rock-encrusted, the floors and ceiling uneven and craggy. Support beams appeared to be stolen phone poles and billboard posts, giving it the look of a derelict coal mine. It was very small and confined, and the threat of claustrophobia dug at me like a creeping itch.

As we walked along, the floor gradually began to decline, until the angle was so severe walking became difficult. We all leaned backward, trying very hard not to fall on our butts and wind up sliding out of control.

"Can we take a break?"

It was Blout, sweaty and out of breath. I was sweating too, my shirt soaked through. "Sure, but let's make it quick."

I wanted to ditch my coat, but needed the things in its pockets: mace, a lock blade, blackjack, a small back-up pistol, and several clips for the .9mm. If I tried to load all that into my pants I'd look like I shit myself.

"How's everybody's head?" I said as I slid down the wall, gripping protruding rocks until I was sitting.

"I'm okay," Blout said.

The ghoul nodded.

I told them I had the Percocet if they needed it, but both waved me off. I felt like a goddamn pusher.

After a minute's rest, Blout signaled he was ready to continue. As soon as I planted my foot for my first step, I fell and immediately began sliding. I held the box with one arm and with the other I grabbed wildly for anything that would stop my skid. Anything turned out to be Blout's pant cuff, and then we were both tumbling out of control down the slope.

The next moment there was nothing beneath us except absolutely black air. As we hurtled downward, all I could do was hold on to the box and brace for impact.

20

The fall was short but painful. I landed with the box under my ribs and heard a loud crunch. Pain shot through my midsection like an electrical charge. I let out a scream that would have shamed Fay Wray. Broken rib for sure, plus I'd aggravated a couple dozen Stockton-inflicted wounds.

The next second I heard Blout hit the ground beside me with a short hard thud. At least his fat ass didn't land on me.

We both stayed on our backs, moaning. Blout was the first to try to get up.

"Are you okay?" he said as he stood, dusting himself off.

I stared up at the ceiling of the tunnel. "Just leave me here. I'll be fine in a day or two."

Blout thought I was kidding. He grabbed my arm and pulled me until I was sitting up. At that point we realized we were now in a huge tunnel, at least twice the width and height of the city's drainage pipe. Then we saw the box. When I fell on it, I'd crushed one side. The hinges had snapped and spilled the beating heart onto the floor. Blout shined the penlight beam on the throbbing muscle. It was filthy with dirt, but still beating.

"Oops."

I gathered it up, wiping it clean with my shirt. Blout watch me tend to the moist hunk of meat with a look of total disgust.

"Maybe after we're done here, you can name it and keep it as a pet," he said and turned away.

I picked a few granules of dirt from one of the sealed arteries then tucked it back into the battered box.

Finally, Mo'Lock appeared, landing feet first and seeming damn pleased about it. He had been there before, but I distinctly recalled that the first time he explored the tunnel he'd arrived on his ass, so his smugness rolled right off me.

"Which way did your buddies go?" I asked.

The ghoul looked slowly in both directions, then back again, and once more to be sure. "Whitney Green is east... that way," he said pointing. "They went west."

"Then west it is." I started to walk, but stopped when I saw Blout holding his head. "What's wrong?"

"It's nothing... just—*NHHHGHGH!*"

The big man buckled and fell. Mo'Lock grabbed

him by the shoulders, catching him before he hit the dirt. I could see the dark glimmer of blood running from both of the cop's nostrils.

I fumbled in my pockets for a pill. Blout was grimacing and shuddering. He was gritting his teeth so hard I could see the pressure was producing blood. It was seeping through the tiny seams between teeth and gum, filling the nooks and crannies with crimson red. Getting him to swallow a pill was going to be tough. I grabbed his face at the jaw and pinched hard, trying to get his teeth to part. It worked on the third squeeze and I jammed the pill in.

It was too late, though. Blout's eyes shot open. They were huge, blazing red with anger. It wasn't Blout—something had him. His body was suddenly animated beyond human capability. His arms flailed as though his limbs had no joints restricting their movement.

Without looking at him, Blout grabbed Mo'Lock by the throat and swung him off the ground, using the ghoul as a weapon against me. He slammed into me, sending the two of us flying hard against the wall.

Mo'Lock and I sprung to our feet and readied for the next attack, but none came. Blout was hanging there in the air, floating before us from invisible puppet strings. I saw blood droplets making mud beneath his feet. Whatever had him planned on killing him. Blood ran from every orifice; the tear ducts in his eyes, his mouth and nose, even from beneath his fingernails.

I stared, not knowing what to do. Something was inside him, manipulating his every move; pushing, pressing, possibly grinding his insides to a pulp. The heart jumped wildly in the box I cradled.

I whispered. "What has him, Mo'?"

"I don't know. I feel Blout and another presence."

Blout's bleeding eyes slammed shut tightly, then abruptly shot open again. His lips parted, allowing foamy blood and a long, lung-clearing hiss to roll out. Although his limbs continued to flail, they were non-threatening movements, like a cutout paper doll blowing in the wind.

I pulled out the .9mm and aimed at the floating cop, with no intention of shooting—yet. Possessed or not, I wouldn't let my friend die without exhausting every last option. I had to wait and let the scene play out.

The noise from Blout's throat changed from its monotone hiss. It began to fluctuate and rise until peaking in a shrill shriek that echoed throughout the tunnel. Mo'Lock winced and covered his ears. Suddenly the noise cut off sharply and fell back to its steady, low hiss. Then, it spoke:

"Get away from this place."

It was a thick, sludgy voice, more like the ghoul's than Blout's. It sounded forced from the gut and past Blout's unwilling, unmoving lips. Only the jaw moved, seeming out of sync with the vocals. The sight reminded me of a strange ventriloquist act.

"Leave here at once and you will be spared!"

I laughed, couldn't help it. As scary as the situation was, the "Great and Powerful Oz" dialogue threw me. Maybe it was the break in the tension, but in that moment I concocted a plan.

The levitating body lurched. "Get out while you still can!"

I flipped the lid off the safe deposit box and scooped out the heart. I let the box drop to the ground, spilling the garnish of charms, stones and herbs. I held the heart tightly in my folded left arm and with my right pressed the 9mm into it. If this thing wanted cornball, I'd give it cornball.

"Let the cop go, or I'll let the heart have it!"

Nothing.

Mo'Lock was staring at me, eyes wide. "Cal, are you sure this is—" he whispered.

"Shut up," I hissed. "It might work."

I stepped forward and pressed the gun harder into the side of the heart and repeated my threat. This time I added a five-second time limit and began the countdown.

Still nothing. I hesitated.

"Four... Three... Two..."

Finally, just when I thought my bluff had been called, Blout dropped limp to the ground. He began coughing and gagging, trying to catch his breath. His wide back heaved and arched as he fought to regain control of his body. He was free, but I knew what'd we'd seen might only be a small taste of the power of our foe.

21

Blout was groggy and agitated, but very much alive. Although the bleeding had been horrible to see, he hadn't lost much blood in the end. It was just enough to achieve the desired effect—scaring the crap out of all of us.

"GHAA! What the hell was that?" Blout sputtered, trying to clear his throat. "I couldn't move, couldn't hear a thing... I was floating in tar."

I tried to help him to his feet, but Blout shook his head. He was still too weak. We all took a seat in the dirt again and ate more painkillers. All except Mo'Lock, who waved me off again.

"You sure?" I said, downing another myself. "How's your head?"

The ghoul nodded confidently. "I'm fine. There's nothing there, I'm sure."

Blout was looking more alert despite the pill. Slowly he came back to his old self. He snapped at me for staring and got annoyed with the blood caked around the various openings of his face. When he got around to re-lighting the cigar he'd dropped I knew he was close to a hundred percent.

I grabbed the box and stood using my free hand to wipe off the dirt that stuck to my pants. It was much more moist than it had been before, less crumbly and more like dough. Definitely doughy. Mo'Lock noticed the same, and was examining one particular wad of the stuff.

"You think we're near water?"

Mo'Lock shook his head slightly. "I don't think this is dirt. Feels like very rich soil."

"Great, we'll start an herb garden."

"I'm no expert, but I thought soil was usually found close to the surface, the top layer."

"Well, add it to the list of weird shit. If there's room."

I started walking on but stopped as Blout grunted and fell behind me. He was injured pretty bad. I began doubting whether he'd be able to continue.

Not that I was much better. With the repeated beating my body was taking, I was asking too much of the painkiller. It couldn't block out pain from injuries and protect me from invading psychic forces forever. Again I thought about the packet in my sock, but fought it off. Not yet, not yet.

We moved along the tunnel, shambling and weaving. The dirt beneath our feet gave in to our every step, adding an unfortunate suction effect that made walking harder. My legs began to ache.

I could make out the rough tunnel walls but not much else—it was just a long dark corridor leading God knew where. I was a little disappointed to see there were no cryptic inscriptions on the walls, no dramatic warnings or symbols to ward off enemies. Then when we came to a turn where I could detect a slight glow of light around the corner.

Blout was beside me. "What the fuck?"

I walked toward the glow, the others following. Blout had his revolver drawn.

The light was dim and yellow, most definitely not natural. It had the erratic blink of a bulb casting twitching shadows in all directions. We slowed as we neared the corner, taking each sticky step carefully. Just before we reached the source of the light, I stepped on something that crinkled.

I grabbed the object from beneath my foot. "You were right, Mo'."

Mo'Lock leaned over my shoulder as I presented an empty plastic bag. The logo was a smirking cartoon cow, with GOOD COW TOP SOIL printed underneath. The ghoul grinned at me. I threw the bag to the ground and moved around the corner.

There were lights lining the hall, scores of naked bulbs hanging from thick bundles of power cords, but they weren't there to illuminate the path. They were grow lights. Countless plants completely covered the tunnel walls, crammed into every inch of space.

The variety of plants was unbelievable, but all were herbs and roots common to all forms of magic and voodoo. Some, like basil and coriander, were common cooking herbs that also had uses in the dark arts. Others were nastier: hemlock, a deadly poison, and a large cluster of the rare aconite plant, also poisonous.

I pointed at the cluster. "Greek legend says that plant came from the mouth of Cerberus..."

"... the dog that guarded the lower world," Mo'Lock nodded and felt the leaf of the plant next to its hood-shaped flower. "Another misplaced myth, a random use of legend and witchcraft."

I slapped his shoulder. "Now you're getting it."

"Not me," Blout spat. "Care to fill me in?"

I held my finger to my mouth. Blout was yelling, and I thought we'd better keep it down. We were close.

"It's been like this throughout the case, Blout. The voodoo charm with the Egyptian symbol, the writings in Cain's books crossing Greek legend with witchcraft, and now this. This plant's Greek origin fits the needs of the perp—to guard this tunnel—but..."

Mo'Lock broke in, "... in reality the plant is used for treating gout and rheumatism."

Blout shook his head violently. "I'm completely lost. Is our perp using stuff wrong because he thinks it's something that it isn't?"

"Maybe, maybe not. It all depends on what you believe."

Blout still didn't understand.

I tried my best to explain, "Some things exist whether we believe in them or not. Like the moon, or the sound of a tree falling in the woods, right?"

Blout blinked once and stared at me.

Mo'Lock took a turn. "But what if something that doesn't exist can be created simply because someone believes in it strongly enough?"

Blout looked from me to Mo'Lock.

"You see what we're getting at?"

"No," Blout said, "I must admit I don't."

Mo'Lock clapped his hands. "It's simple. The power of belief can create things which might not exist, granting them power and making them real."

Blout glared at the ghoul for a long time. "Let me tell you what I believe, freak job. I believe this is getting too damn weird, and after what happened to me back there, we need some backup. That would be the smart play."

I said, "If you're getting scared, you're welcome to hang back and wait."

"Don't pull that kiddy crap with me!" Blout growled. "And I'm not scared."

Blout stomped forward. As we continued on our way our surroundings began to change. The tunnel narrowed and the plants thinned to one every several feet.

As Blout rounded a bend, I heard him retch violently and hurried to catch up. Our path was blocked. A pair of disembodied heads sat impaled on a two-pronged spike protruding from the soft ground. Based on the torn flesh and dangling veins at the neck, they had been violently ripped from their bodies. I didn't need Mo'Lock to tell me that these were his missing buddies, but he did just the same.

"It's them, Cal. It's them."

I began to raise my arm to the ghoul's shoulder but stopped when the heads simultaneously snapped open their eyes.

"Mo'Lock, is that you?" the left head said. Its voice was hollow, accompanied by a deep sucking sound that whistled through the open end of its neck.

We all took a step back. Blout was making the sign of the cross.

Mo'Lock recovered from the initial shock and quickly stepped towards the heads. "Tyus," Mo'Lock said addressing the left head, "what happened?"

Tyus blinked once and tried to wet his lips. It was futile. "We failed. Attacked by a mob of zombie hooligans. Please forgive us."

Mo'Lock placed his hand to his chest and for a moment I thought he would weep. "No. Forgive me. I should not have sent you. Where are your bodies? What did they do with them?"

The head on the right spoke. "They burned them before our eyes and set our heads here with a warning." The ghoul head turned his eyes to me. "The warning was for you, Cal McDonald. Stay away, or certain death awaits."

I shrugged and spat. "Whatever. Who gave you that message? Cain himself?"

Tyus spoke again. "It was just a voice."

"In our heads."

I looked at Mo'Lock. "Do you want to go back and get them to safety?

Your call."

The heads spoke together. "We'll be fine. Go and stop this thing. This place stinks of death."

The right head made an effort to look past the ghoul and me. "I think your human friend could use some help."

Mo'Lock and I turned to find Blout out cold, spread eagle on his back. God, how I envied him. He'd get to sleep through it all.

The ghoul and I kept going, leaving Blout with the heads and the message that we'd pressed on. I sensed we were close as the heart beat hard inside the box. Whatever Cain had begun or become, it was soon time for a showdown. I was eager to get it over with. My only regret was that I'd miss the look on Blout's face when the heads gave him our message.

22

The long corridor became thinner and thinner as Mo'Lock and I advanced. The lights here were spotty and dim, only a few every other yard or so to accommodate a plant here, a root there. Still, there was enough light to see that the end was a long way off. At least I could see no immediate threats. The only sounds were our own footfalls grinding in the soft, muddy dirt and the occasional drag and kick when one of us lost our footing.

The peace and quiet bothered me more than the action. It gave me time to feel my hurting body, each and every cut, scrape and bruise. I was a mass of pain and needed the distraction of motion. Without it, the pain was too much. I couldn't focus. It was then, I think, that my mind was first tugged away...

All at once, my head began to feel strange. It hit like a breeze, then a

wave, building to the force of a wrecking ball. Not pain, not really, more like a creeping paralysis—like a stiff, aching joint. I had to stop. I was confused, unsure where I was.

"Cal, are you all right?" a voice said to my side.

I couldn't see anything. Was I home. Too late?

The voice repeated the question.

I covered my face in my hands. "Yeah, I'm fine, Dad..."

"What?" Mo'Lock asked.

I felt his hand on my shoulder. "I said I'm..."

I blinked, shaking my confusion away as I dug in my pocket for a pill. The bitter crunch was a needed slap in the face. My vision cleared and I saw the ghoul standing there with a look of unmistakable worry.

"Stop that," I said, standing fully erect. "Fucking ghoul."

I walked away stamping my feet and used my tongue to pick at the jagged chunks of pill stuck in my teeth. Behind me Mo'Lock had a hand to his temple and a strained expression on his stiff white face.

"What's up?" I asked, but didn't slow my stride.

The ghoul kept walking brow raised. "I just had the oddest sensation," he said. "It was as though my brain itched."

"I'm tellin' you, take a fucking pill."

"No. The alcohol is still doing the job. I feel sufficiently bleary."

"Mo'Lock—"

"Cal. No. I can do this, and you've got a job to do."

He wasn't going to budge. It was that uncanny ability to stay focused. He didn't want me to worry or get distracted. No matter how badly I treated him, I was always his number one priority. I thought about it all the time. He could have any life he wanted, even travel the world if he so desired, yet here he was slopping through a subterranean voodoo pit with me—with not so much as a complaint.

"Cal. Up ahead."

Ten feet in front of us, a zombie stood frozen, legs bent and poised to attack, its empty eye sockets dripping oily maggots. One hand was braced on the craggy earth, the other fanned out with palm toward us.

"Shit. Only one?" I laughed.

I handed Mo'Lock the heart and started in, but the thing wasn't looking for a fight. I'd called its bluff. When I got within striking distance, it spun away and ran off into the darkness.

When I turned back to Mo'Lock to gloat, my stomach sank.

Hanging between me and the ghoul was the body of a man, swinging by his broken neck. I backed away, forcing myself to look up at the twisted face. Fuck if I hadn't seen it before. It was my father as I'd found him years before; blue-faced, bloated tongue sticking out grotesquely between tight lips.

I spun away, letting a cry escape, but a new obstacle blocked my way. I covered my eyes, but this only left my other senses open to attack.

"Calvin? Is that you?" The voice was soft and tiny. I remembered it instantly despite the years. Then I smelled baby powder and knew she was there.

I spread the fingers covering my eyes and saw her standing there as beautiful as the last day I saw her—my sister Stephie. Seven years old and so pretty, the image of my mother.

"Stephie! Yes, honey, it's me... Cal." I heard my voice cracking. I was losing control. It's not her, I told myself. I clamped my eyes tightly shut and tried to speak, but before I could, Stephie's face changed from the sweet child I'd known to one filled with burning rage.

"Why weren't you in the car, Cal?" she spat. Crevices began to appear across her forehead, blood filling the hairline cracks. "You were supposed to be in the car. Me and mom waited, but you never came."

I shook my head hard and beat myself with my fist. The image before me flickered. "Get out of my head!" I screamed and struck myself again.

Stephie was falling apart. Blood ran from her face

as it was raked to the bone by an invisible shattered windshield. She cried my name and called out to our father hanging from the rope. I slammed my head again and screamed, pulling my hair.

"Get out!"

As quickly as they'd come, the images disappeared.

"Fuck!" I slammed my fist into the tunnel wall. I was mad and needed a release. I thought I'd break my hand for sure, but the wall turned out not to be stone and rock at all. The soft red clay fell in a spray of chunks when my fist hit it.

"What now? Mo'Lock!"

"I beg your pardon, sir?"

The voice was the ghoul's, but distinctly different. The hoarse grumble was gone, the imaginary echo no longer there. It was a clear, proper voice. I took a closer look at him. He stood complete and upright, the rigid stance of a gentleman of long ago.

"What is this place? A mine shaft? Where are Caroline and the children?"

I stuttered. I didn't know what to say. It wasn't my ghoul that stood in the tunnel with me. It wasn't anybody I'd ever known.

"Oh, do speak up man! Where are my wife and children?"

"What year is it... sir?" I asked trying to sound polite.

The man was indignant. "Are you daft? It's December 15th, 1919," he spat, looking around the tunnel. "Now answer my question. Where are my wife an—"

He cut himself off and banged his head with his big bony hands. *"NGGGH!* Leave me... get out of my mind!"

It was Mo'Lock's voice, but it didn't last seven words.

The gentleman came back, but the pompousness was gone. This time his face was dreamy, unaware of his surroundings. His eyes were welling with tears.

"Caroline dear, I promise you the automobile is perfectly safe, perfectly safe."

I stepped toward the weeping ghoul. "Mo'Lock, are you..."

The gentleman became unsettled as I approached. "My... my name is Michael Locke. Can't you see that I've killed my family?"

That was all I could take. I hauled off and let the ghoul have it right in the side of the head. He reeled backwards and I saw his face change. We stood there silent as Mo'Lock wiped the tears away from his face, studying them before wiping his hands on his pants.

"Thank you, Cal."

I looked at him a long moment. "Looks like you and I share something."

The ghoul nodded. "We always have."

Now I really wanted to kill whatever was at the end of the tunnel. I wanted it to suffer, suffer like it made us suffer. I knew the pain Mo'Lock carried was as great as my own and that was fuel, baby—fuel that would bring this evil down hard.

Just then I noticed the place on the wall where a chunk of clay had fallen after I'd hit it. The naked patch was about the size of a jar lid, a glistening moist whiteness beneath the surface of the clay. It reminded me of the flesh of a floater, a drowning victim that has been in the water for days.

I gave the patch a prod with my index finger. It was cold, soft and clammy and caved at my touch. A shudder ran through my body, echoed by a soft roll that seemed to travel through the ground beneath our feet. I realized then why it reminded me of the flesh of a drowned person. It was human skin.

And unlike a floater, it was alive.

23

I kicked the dirt at my feet and revealed another fleshy white patch. We were so busy trying to get to the end of the tunnel that it never dawned on us that the thing we sought was the tunnel itself. At some point we had entered it and never knew.

It was time to make a move before whatever Cain had become tried to get in our heads again. The surrounding blubbery wall gave me an idea. It was time to get drastic. I shot a look at Mo'Lock.

"Let's fuck this thing up."

I tried not to think about the clammy flesh surrounding us. The idea that we might be inside some gigantic monstrosity was too disgusting to consider. I pushed the thought out of my mind by retrieving the pouch from my sock. I pulled out the needle, spoon, syringe, and last, but hardly least, the packet of chunky white power.

I created a little torch out of some debris, stuck it into the dirt and lit it. Then I put the chunk into the spoon and spit on it several times. The drugs and saliva cooked over the candle flame until they melted.

I filled the needle, pushing the plunger to clear out the air bubbles. A major overdose was on the way.

Mo'Lock knelt down beside me. "Cal, are you sure you want to do this? Aren't the pills working?"

I grinned and gave the needle a little squirt. "Who said it was for me? Let me have the heart. I'm gonna try a little voodoo magic myself... with a twist of smack."

I pinned the heart to the dirt with my left hand. The muscle began beating harder, fighting me. The walls and floor began to shudder and rumble. The thing was getting jumpy.

I wasted no more time. I raised the needle in my right hand and jabbed

it into the center of the heart, emptying all but a single hit of heroin into the pulsing muscle. Instantly the heart fluttered and beat hard, then settled down to a slow, steady pace.

A low moan echoed through the tunnel like a powerful generator grinding to a slow halt. The sound came from all sides, even from inside my head for a flash.

I took what was left of the smack, enough to overdose an elephant, and stabbed the fleshy patch on the wall. I didn't know how big the thing was, so I couldn't guess how long the drugs would last, but I definitely wanted to err on the side of safety. The bellowing moan sounded again, louder this time. When the floor rumbled violently, I left the needle dangling from the wall, grabbed the heart and Mo'Lock and ran for the end of the tunnel.

At the tunnel's mouth, zombies blocked the path. Their empty eye sockets panned back and forth, waiting for us to come at them.

The ghoul and I slowed, but we didn't stop. When the zombies saw that we weren't going to turn back, they scattered, clearing a path for us. They were all bluff and wouldn't risk a fight, since we were aware of their vulnerability.

We entered a massive room the size of an aircraft hanger, but more square than rectangle. The walls were parts of many things; red clay, hard rock, and stone. Protruding everywhere, ceiling to floor, was bone-white skin, throbbing and moist. We moved into the center of the room, surrounded by fires tended by zombies. They kept their distance, cowering and shielding the talismans around their necks with bony hands.

Behind me, Mo'Lock was staring in awe at the fleshy room. There was a tangible energy in here I was sure he felt. It made every tiny hair on my body stand on end.

Familiar symbols covered every exposed surface, while altars occupied the lower halves of three walls. One I recognized as a classic voodoo altar, covered with dried blood and melted candles, copper pots overflowing with chicken feet. Another appeared more satanic, with a Hand of Glory—the severed hand of a suicide victim—placed in front of a goat's head. The third was a clean white table combining the symbols of the Jewish, Christian, Hindu, and Muslim religions.

But the fourth wall was where I found what we'd been chasing all along, the source of perhaps a thousand deaths. A thing that had once been a nothing, a nobody. A little man who decided to take whatever he needed to invent his own world. He created a reality by pick-pocketing the beliefs of the world and using it to recreate himself as a monster that fed on brains, the very source of the soul. By doing so, he'd made his own world.

It was an unbelievable testament to the power of belief and the ugliness of egotism and hatred. Why is it when humans tap into tremendous power, the first instinct for most is to take, to destroy? Before me was just another example of someone who could have been special, the greatest intellect on earth, but instead used his power to shed blood and sow terror.

I stared at the face in the wall—the face was the

wall. It was gnarled by rock and stone, stretched by its own voracious appetite. It looked stupefied by the heroin flowing through its massive system.

It was a face I knew and suspected, but one I still couldn't quite believe I was seeing again.

This was the reason I did what I did. This was a monster.

"Hello Cain. It's been a long time."

24

Staring at the abomination, my mind raced back to the aftermath of our last confrontation. I'd stood watching them hose off the street, the gooey pink gripping the asphalt, desperately fighting to hold its ground. But the hoses won in the end, and bit by splattered slimy bit, the last remains of Edgar Cain were washed into the sewers.

Unfortunately, Cain had a back-up plan. His heart lived on in the deposit box, and as long as the heart lived, so did he. After that, he had all the time in the world to perfect the powers of his abnormal brain, using his own strange blend of religion and magic. Finally he could populate his lonely existence, and eventually reanimate his own splattered, defeated form.

I scanned the room and saw pink-white flesh protruding everywhere from clay and rock. How deep was this fucking head embedded in the earth? How many lives stolen in their sleep? And that terrible force...

I had to remind myself that if I killed Cain once, I

could do it again. This time, there would be no coming back.

"I wouldn't phink pho loud if I were yoo, Detective."

The face was speaking. And it sounded as though the drugs were working. He was trashed.

"Okay, then I'll say it out loud. You're going down, Cain," I said. "You've done enough killing for one lifetime."

Cain's eyes blinked sluggishly. "I'ph kilt no one. I absorbed the lonely... the ill... the hopeleph." He blinked again and smacked his lips trying to shake the effects of the drugs.

Mo'Lock stepped up beside my right shoulder. "Actually, Mr. Cain, you did far worse than killing them. You stole their souls, their essence. You took what little chance many of these people had for eternal peace."

The face guffawed. "Nonsense! You know nophing!"

I stepped toward Cain's face. "It's over. Face it, you're done."

My confidence infuriated the giant head even more, but he was too wasted to fully react. "W...why you... Do you know what you are dealing with?! I am the second giant! I could bend and break you with a

174

single thought! I am the single biggest intellect in all the world!"

It was time to act. I held the throbbing heart out so that the face could see it clearly. "Recognize this?"

Cain's eyes widened. "How did you f...find it?"

I stepped back. "Brown corduroy bell bottoms. The key in the wallet. I just followed the corduroy road."

Cain wasn't as upset as I would have thought, but there was still serious worry in his eyes. Then he squeezed his lids tightly shut, and for a moment a dull image flickered in my mind. Stephie again, bloody and begging for help. This time, the image quickly faded.

Cain coughed, blinked and clamped his eyes shut again.

This time there was a suggestion, a lame imitation of my inner voice telling me to shoot myself. I shook my head and flipped it off like a bronco throwing a quadriplegic.

I tapped my right foot and bobbled the heart hand to hand. "Are you finished?"

I threw the organ to the floor. It flopped once, rolled and came to rest underneath Cain's chin. Now it was my turn to do the glaring. I stared it right in the eyes and waited for its worry to turn to fear. To speed up the process, I took out both of my pistols, the six shot in my left and the .9mm in my right.

Cain snorted. "I'ph grown beyond my heart. Go ahead."

"We'll see."

Cain's eyes met mine. Now tears welled in the stretched corners. "Please... don't..."

I sneered. "Kiss my ass."

I went into my best Two Gun Kid imitation, firing both guns from the hip and making that beating heart dance.

Cain screamed with the sound of a thousand voices.

The heart blew apart into a splattered mess of tissue and goo, a hundred bloody chunks. I kept firing until there were a thousand, reloaded and shot until I had to reload again. The heart was a grease mark when I finished. A crimson smear.

While I reloaded, I noticed Mo'Lock going berserk.

He had smashed one altar and was on to the next, using a steel candle stand as a weapon. Hit by crushing hit, he was destroying everything in sight.

"... please, stop... please!" Cain pleaded to deaf ears.

He screamed and begged and howled for help that would never come. Or so I thought.

Because right then, I heard three clicking sounds

behind me. Mo'Lock and I turned in unison, raising our hands as we swiveled. It was a reflex. You always reach for the sky when you have guns pointed at you.

At the mouth of the chamber stood Randy, Scott and Miriam—the Frankenteens. Each held an M-16, and they all wore a look of condescending "I-screwed-you" pleasure that made my stomach twist in a knot so hard it actually hurt.

"Motherfuckers."

Cain giggled at our backs. Randy raised his weapon and stepped forward.

"You're the motherfucker, McDonald," he spat. "You're the one who took everything away from us!"

I glanced at the ghoul, utterly shocked at the sight of him. His eyes were wide, blazing. I'd seen him angry before, but this? This was different. It sent a chill down my spine.

I kept my hands raised. "I tried to help you kids. How was I supposed to know you were as messed up as Lazar." I pointed a thumb back towards Cain. "And I don't even want to know how you got hooked up with this loser!"

Randy twitched angrily and squeezed off a shot at my feet. Cain squealed. Randy shot again, and this time he hit me right in the same goddamn spot he'd shot me the first time! I reeled back and screamed. It hurt like a bitch.

Scott and Miriam looked nervous.

"Mr. Cain contacted us," Scott said. "In our heads."

Miriam smacked Scott in the chest. "Shut up!"

Randy moved forward again.

"The next one goes through your head, McDonald!" He yelled and raised the M-16 as promised.

I didn't even see Mo'Lock take the gun out of the kid's hands. It was that fast. Then the ghoul stood over Randy, his face twisted in such a grotesque sculpture of rage that I hardly recognized him.

"You lied to me."

That was all he said before proceeding to dismember Randy limb from limb. He ripped the kid's arms from their sockets effortlessly. Skin tore with a rubbery snap and bones popped with a sickening crunch. In a matter of seconds, Randy was returned to the pile of miscellaneous organs and limbs he'd been in Dr. Polynice's Lab.

Then Mo'Lock turned to the other two.

They shot at him as he marched. He took the bullets right in the chest but kept on advancing steadily. After they'd been disarmed he tore them apart as he had their leader, without making a single sound. It was the most terrifying thing I'd ever witnessed in my life, and I've seen quite a lot, thank you. I was never happier to count Mo'Lock as a friend. Plus, I learned an invaluable lesson—never lie to a ghoul.

When he was finished, arms and legs were scattered all over the chamber floor. I could see Mo'Lock took no pleasure in what he'd done. Regardless, I gave him a nod. He paused and returned the gesture.

I looked up to Cain triumphantly. "Got anything else?"

Cain smirked, and the chamber began to rock.

Mo'Lock and I stood in place, dumbfounded. We were out of options. The heart was obliterated, but Edgar Cain still lived. He'd actually become powerful enough to do without his heart. Cain's eyes glowed with renewed malevolence as his wide lips parted and he spoke the words that were running through my mind.

"You are so screwed."

The walls shook, throbbing as the heart once had. Clay and stone loosened and crumbled, crashing down around our heads.

I rolled away from the falling debris, reloading the 9mm and revolver as I moved. I tossed a gun to Mo'Lock who just stared at it.

"What am I supposed to do with this?" A gigantic

wedge of damp red clay landed at his side. He didn't even flinch.

"Just shoot!"

Cain's eyes spun in his head. "No!"

I raised my gun into the air and fired once. Above us the fleshy surface burst open as the slug impacted, and gooey pink matter spat out in violent, gushing bursts. I looked at Mo'Lock and he gave me an affirmative nod. We'd get out of this mess yet.

"Looks like this baby's about to blow," I said. "What say we help it along?"

Cain began screaming again, trying anything to distract me. When I felt him pulling at my brain, I shook my head, leveled the .9mm at his distended face and fired twice. The skin parted slightly where the bullet struck, but there was no blood.

Nothing.

But deep inside the head, the pressure was building, pushing at the small hole until it split and ripped lengthwise. Before I could react, a geyser of snotty pink goo shot across my face.

I dove, rolled to one knee and picked up one of the Frankenteens' M-16s, unleashing a blaze of automatic fire into the right wall. Behind me, the ghoul was shooting in dangerously random directions. Each shot brought forth a gusher of crude pink brain matter.

The fleshy walls rumbled and shook, percolating like bags of boiling tar. And then the smell wafted into my nostrils. I gagged, my stomach lurching. The stench was worse than death, hot and thick, and impossible to ignore.

Cain was finally silent.

His forehead spit pink and gray, his eyes teared, and saliva-soaked lips blubbered uncontrollably. I almost felt sorry for him. Almost, but not quite.

Mo'Lock and I met in the center of the room, dodging falling slabs of clay and rock. A growing roar rumbled ominously inside. On the ceiling and walls, tiny geysers of matter tore at the small holes, enlarging them.

I looked down at my feet and saw we were already ankle deep in fetid soup. Edgar Cain's eyes were closed, but tears ran freely through closed lids.

"Cain," I said. My tone was soft, almost a whisper.

The face opened its eyes.

I leveled the M-16, point blank, between his eyes. "In your next life, get out of the house more often."

I emptied the clip into his face, killing him once and for all. Unfortunately, I also opened the brain matter floodgates. The gunk had now risen to our knees, and all around us the flesh walls were stretched to breaking. The evil was finally dead, but so were Mo'Lock and me if we didn't make tracks quickly.

Mo'Lock looked at me. "Got a plan?"

I nodded. "Run."

25

Running knee-deep in the thick, ever-increasing brain matter proved easier said than done. I could hardly move, let alone raise my legs above the slop. At least Mo'Lock had a height advantage. He used it to jump free of the current and gain about a half yard each time. I had to push my way through, which considering the shape I was in was no simple task.

By the time he reached the tunnel, I was still several yards behind. The head pudding was now waist high and the walls and ceiling threatened to burst. If it cut loose before I got to Mo'Lock, I'd had it for sure.

Lucky for me, the ghoul's loyalty was stronger than his own sense of self-preservation. When he saw I was having a hard time, he cut through the flowing gunk with relative ease, grabbed my wrist and headed back to the exit. The fact that he was dragging an extra hundred and ninety pounds with him had little effect on the ghoul.

Just as we reached the exit, the far wall split with a thunderous tear. A tidal wave of brain rushed into the room. Steam rolled off the bubbling surface, producing a new eye-searing wave of stench. It was like a slaughterhouse in August filled with rotten eggs, bad cottage cheese and just a hint of old foot. Mo'Lock gagged. I tried to draw air through my mouth, but it was little help.

At the exit, the streaming brains were causing a nasty undercurrent. One moment Mo'Lock and I were gripping the walls of the tunnel, the next we were swept away, riding the wild pink gunk. Behind us, I heard another flesh wall swell and burst, and the speed of the rapids pulled us along even faster. I tried to grab hold of the walls, but it was hopeless. We were moving too fast and it took all my energy to keep my head above the torrent. I figured the tunnel would fill and either rake our heads along the ceiling or simply drown us. Either way, it was looking mighty grim.

The surface in front of me bubbled, foamed, and broke. Stinking pink muck spattered, blinding me momentarily. When I managed to clear my vision, Mo'Lock was right in front of me, his sight seemingly unaffected by the fumes. He must have swam backward to find me. He threw his long arm around my neck, pulled me close and helped me stay above the current.

"Hang on!" the ghoul yelled.

"I'm trying!" I screamed back, "But I think I left my Palm Pilot back there!"

"Shut up and save your breath, Cal!"

We were traveling through the tunnel at three times the rate we had walked in. It was difficult to tell where we were, save for the fact there was now little more than a foot and a half of air separating us from the jagged ceiling. The thick current tugged and pulled at our legs, slamming us side to side against the tunnel walls. Mo'Lock did his best to hold onto me, but the constant pounding made the task next to impossible.

Twice he lost me, only to grab me again. The second time, I went under and got a mouthful of grotesque, gelatinous head pudding. I choked and almost swallowed. I thought I'd drown in the crap for sure, but somehow I forced the slime from my mouth, shut my eyes tight and held my breath. I thought I'd try to ride it out, hold on until the tunnel ended at Whitney Green. Maybe there the pink sludge would spill into the burnt foundation of the building and I would find air.

Then I felt a hand grabbing at my hair, followed by a painful yank that removed several clumps of hair. I gasped and gulped greedily—fresh air. Mo'Lock had pulled me to the surface. I spat and choked, trying to clear my eyes and ears.

"Cal!" The voice screamed.

It was Blout just ahead of us, sounding closer by the second.

I screamed. "Blout! Over here!"

"Up ahead, Cal! My hand! My hand! Can you see it?!"

I tried to focus through one eye. Ahead was the point where we fell into the tunnel. I could just make out a dark object swinging back and forth from the ceiling.

"See it?" Mo'Lock yelled at my ear.

"I think so." I blinked my eyes hard. The slime was stubborn and sticky. Finally, I was able to make out the fuzzy outline of Blout's hand hanging down just yards from me and closing fast. "I see it!"

There was another surge of brains. We were thrown against the left wall of the tunnel and a second swell almost scraped our heads against the ceiling. Mo'Lock pulled me closer, then moved his hand to the back of my shirt and held on like a mother cat holds a kitten's scruff. I could see Blout's hand dangling from an unseen ledge.

Mo'Lock strained to hold me further above the pink and gray rapids. "Grab hold, Cal! Grab hold of his hand!"

Blout was screaming as well. He couldn't see us,

so he had no idea I was about to hit. I hoped the sudden jolt didn't drag him over the edge.

"I'm here!" I warned. I saw his fingers flex and spread wide, ready to grab hold.

Another second, another swell of brain and our hands met. Blout had me. But Mo'Lock was slipping. I reached with my free hand, grabbed for his suit coat and got it, but the rapids threw and twisted him and the collar tore.

"Mo'Lock!" I cried out, dangling in the air.

Blout pulled me out of the torrent. As I hit dry ground I got a glimpse of Mo'Lock being taken away by the rapids. He flailed his arms and yelled something I couldn't make out. Then he was gone.

26

I was on solid ground. I rose to my knees and pounded my fist on the dirt. "Damn!"

Blout was right there beside me. "Christ, are you all right?"

I felt his hand on my shoulder, and swung my head around to face the big man. I was pumped. I must have looked like a rabid dog, but this thing wasn't over. I had to stay pumped or I'd drop like a rag doll.

Blout's slacks were wet from the knees down. He'd gotten himself out before the tunnel filled. "How'd you get up here?"

He shook his head. "I didn't. I found a manhole back a ways. I climbed out there, doubled back and came here," he said, impressed with himself. "What the hell happened down there?"

"You don't want to know, trust me," I said. "But Cain's dead."

Blout jumped. "You sure this time?"

I nodded and started walking away. "It ain't over yet. We've got to get to Whitney Green." I stopped, and turned. "Did you get the heads?"

Blout shuddered visibly, but nodded. "I left them at the entrance."

"Thanks. You're a pal."

Outside the tunnel I picked up the heads. Blout had wrapped them in his jacket, and they were pleased to hear the danger had passed. I told them what had happened and they were as anxious as I was to rescue Mo'Lock.

"Mo'Lock's as tough as they come," said the head called Tyus. "I'm sure he's fine."

I wasn't so sure, but agreed anyway.

Blout stood by, watching me converse with the two disembodied heads with an air of absolute disgust. Then he went to his car to radio for backup. I heard him mention Whitney Green. I didn't like it. I had to get there before any cops did.

I ran to the road. Cars were whizzing by in pre-rush hour panic. I tucked the bundled heads under my left arm, and with my right waved to passing taxis. Blout was yelling as a cab screeched to a halt. I ignored him. I opened the back door of the cab and tossed in the bundle as Blout ran towards me.

I waved him off. "Wait for the backup. Meet me at the Green."

The driver was a ghoul as I'd hoped, so I explained the situation to him. He knew Mo'Lock and understood the immediacy of the dilemma. He burned rubber and we headed toward Whitney Green at seventy miles an hour. I introduced the heads as I unwrapped them, but the driver already knew 'em. Cozy community.

Ten minutes later we came to a screeching halt just outside the entrance of Whitney Green. I shot out of the cab without paying, leaving the severed heads behind. The driver agreed to take care of them. I didn't know exactly what that meant, but then again I didn't care.

"Just save Mo'Lock," he told me. "That would be payment enough."

I sprinted to the edge of the burnt pit that was once Cain's home. Now it was a huge hole, bubbling and foaming with slimy, surging brain matter. It spread out before me like a lake of frothy, stinking pulp. I scanned the surface for any sign of movement among the floating debris. There was nothing.

A horrible sinking feeling began to well in my gut. I felt panicky. Where the fuck was Mo'Lock?!

I could hear sirens wailing in the distance and closing fast. When the cops saw this, they'd do their best to cover it up, meaning I sure as shit didn't want to be there. I got panicky. Pacing the edge of the hole, I cupped my hands and began to yell.

"MOOOO'LOCK!" I hollered and repeated even louder, *"MOOO'LOCK!"*

From the shadows somewhere behind me, a figure shifted. "I'm not deaf, you know. I'm right here."

I spun on my heels. Mo'Lock stepped from the shadows, dripping pink slime.

I ran over to him, grabbed him by the shoulders, and shook him. "You crazy fucking ghoul! You scared the crap out of me!"

Mo'Lock smiled.

"Don't get the wrong idea, gruesome." I could feel the adrenaline fading quickly and all the pain beginning to return. "I just need someone to get me to the hospital."

27

I dreamt about terrible pain shooting through my ass, and being chased by rolling dumpsters overflowing with decapitated heads. After that, I woke in a hospital room bandaged from head to toe. The blinds were closed and the room was dark. I could see my arm was in a support, dangling above my bandaged torso. Beside me I heard beeping apparatus that I suspected did little more than raise the per day rate.

My head was wrapped in bandages and gauze so thick that I could hardly lift it to see whether I was alone. I used every ounce of strength to raise my head off the pillow and was rewarded with the sight of a lumpy figure slumped in a chair next to the window. It was Blout, fast asleep.

With a great deal of effort I got my hand on the bedpan so comfortably rammed under my ass. I dragged it out to the edge of the bed where I let it fall to the ground. There was huge clanging noise. Blout shot to his feet, reaching frantically for his holster. I had just enough energy to chuckle. Then I passed out again. This time, I dreamt of nothing, and that was fine by me.

*   *   *

I woke later and found Blout still in the room with me. He was asleep again, but now light seeped in at the corners of the closed shades. I dragged my head to the edge of the mattress and saw a mountain of crumbled fast-food bags and crushed coffee cups on the floor.

Christ. How long had I been out?

"Who do you have to fuck to get a drink around here?"

Blout stirred. When he stood I could see that he had a large, square bandage on the left side of his forehead. A spotty blotch of dried brown blood showed through. His hands were wrapped with bandages, but in a way that gave most of his fingers freedom to move.

"You ain't fucking me no more this week. I've had enough."

His face was stone. I waited for the explosion. Instead I got a big toothy grin.

"Welcome back, asshead." He slapped my leg. It hurt. "You had us scared for a while there. You know they had to pump your damn stomach?"

Then the big guy reached into his overcoat and pulled a small stuffed rabbit that had a "Get Well Soon" sign. "Here, I bought you this fuckin' bunny."

The bunny landed next to me, rolled and fell on its cute little face. I tried to sit up, but quit after a brief and futile attempt. "How long was I out?"

"I think it's a record for you. Almost four days. Today is the fourth day, but it's early."

"Damn." I was impressed. "Everything turn out okay?"

"Yeah, it seems there was some kind of weird spill at the burned out Whitney Green apartments. I called out the Hazmat crew and they gathered what they could, destroyed what they gathered and burned what was left in the pit." Blout had a big grin plastered across his face.

I snickered and felt my ribs throb. "What about the media?"

Blout laughed again. "You kidding? Chemical spills are the one thing that keeps their asses out of our business. Nobody knows nothing about nothing."

"But you're keeping the file open?"

"Damn right. I'm not about to report the case closed. I am not going to put myself in a situation where I have to explain what happened down there." He was shaking his head.

I grinned and pulled my arm out of the sling, trying again to sit up. This time Blout helped me and I made it. "What's the matter, Blout? Afraid nobody will believe you?"

"Exactly. I'll leave that crap to you."

I nodded. We both ran out of witty banter, and fell quiet. It was a little uncomfortable.

"It's over, isn't it, Cal?" Blout said, low and quiet.

I nodded. "Definitely."

"You're sure this time?"

I glared. "Absolutely."

Blout stuck his big hand out in front of my face. "That was real good work you did. Thank you."

I took his hand and shook it. There would have been another awkward silence, but the door was pushed opened by a scurrying male nurse, followed by the doctor. A heartbeat later, Mo'Lock lumbered in wearing a spiffy new suit.

Blout shot a look at the ghoul, then quickly back to me. "I've got to get going," he said and shook my hand again. "I'll check back before they let you go."

I thought Blout would go to great lengths to avoid Mo'Lock, but as he passed by the ghoul he gave him a slap on the shoulder.

Mo'Lock waited patiently while the doctor and nurse checked me out. When they had gone, he made sure the door was shut. He turned and tossed me a little stuffed rabbit much like the one Blout had given me.

"All my friends are comedians," I said.

Mo'Lock smiled. "Pull its head off."

"What?"

"Pull the head off."

I gave the bunny head a twist and pull. It came off with a pop, exposing the neck of a half pint of good stinky hooch. I grinned and looked up at the ghoul. "God bless you."

"I figured you'd have a bad case of the DTs when you woke up."

"Naw, they've got me pretty pumped full of juice. I don't feel a thing."

The ghoul stepped around to the foot of the bed and lifted my chart off the hook, scanning it with big, dead eyes. After a second, he let out a long whistle. "Four hundred stitches. That a record?"

"Yeah, I'm breaking them left and right. Where's my goddamn trophy? So what's been going on while I was in la-la land?"

The ghoul touched his hand to his chin. "Surprisingly quiet, really. The lawyer for the man who was suing you left a message with a new court date. I wrote it down."

"Great. Enjoying my apartment?"

"Yes, thank you. Landlord stopped by. He said he wants you to pay for the front door. He left a bill. The insurance co—"

I waved him off. "Okay, okay. What about work? I need some cash—a lot of cash—and I need it yesterday."

Mo'Lock stood at the foot of the bed staring at me for a moment, as if he was deciding whether or not he should tell me anything that might get me excited. Then he took out a small spiral memo book, flipped it open and began to read.

"We got a call this morning from…"

"We?"

"You got a call from a woman named Veronica Vanderbilt."

"As in the 'we-got-more-money-than-anyone-in-the-world' Vanderbilts?"

"The one and only." The ghoul went on. "She sounded very scared and would like you to come to the house as soon as possible."

I was feeling better by the second. "What's the skinny?"

"She has a teenage son who is acting very strange. Sleeps all day and stays out all night."

I shrugged. "Sounds like a teenager to me."

"This morning she said she found something in the boy's closet that alarmed her. She didn't want to call the police. She was too embarrassed, so she called you."

"What was in the closet?" I rolled my eyes, pretending I didn't see the answer coming up Main Street.

Together we said, "A coffin."

I nodded. "What'd you say my... our rate was?"

Mo'Lock grinned. "A grand a day plus expenses."

"Sounds good. Now help me out of this fucking bed." I tipped the headless bunny into my mouth and emptied it, then got shakily to my feet. There was no time to waste. We had a new case.